"I want you in my bed."

Pierce's eyes glittered with desire. "And I can guarantee you wouldn't feel *empty*—far from it!"

It was obvious the comment she had once made about him had hurt more than he had shown at the time, and the insult had been far from forgotten.

"Emotionally, I would," she answered softly. "And that's what's important."

Pierce's mouth twisted. "If you think that in time I'll fall in love with you, you're in for a great disappointment."

Danny shook her head sadly. "I'm hoping I'll fall in love with you, because that's the only reason I'd ever make love with you. It wouldn't be making love otherwise, would it?"

He suddenly drew in a ragged breath. "Don't let me hurt you, Danielle."

"I won't have the choice. It's a risk one takes."

CAROLE MORTIMER one of our most popular—and prolific—English authors, began writing for the Harlequin Presents series in 1979. She now has more than forty top-selling romances to her credit and shows no signs whatsoever of running out of plot ideas. She writes strong traditional romances with a distinctly modern appeal, and her winning way with characters and romantic plot twists has earned her an enthusiastic audience worldwide.

Books by Carole Mortimer

HARLEQUIN PRESENTS

These books may be available at your local bookseller.

Don't miss any of our special offers. Write to us at the following address for information on our newest releases.

Harlequin Reader Service
901 Fuhrmann Blvd., P.O. Box 1397, Buffalo, NY 14240
Canadian address: P.O. Box 2800, Postal Station A,
5170 Yonge St., Willowdale, Ont. M2N 6J3

CAROLE MORTIMER

darkness into light

Harlequin Books

TORONTO • NEW YORK • LONDON
AMSTERDAM • PARIS • SYDNEY • HAMBURG
STOCKHOLM • ATHENS • TOKYO • MILAN

For John
Matthew and Joshua

Harlequin Presents first edition June 1986
ISBN 0-373-10892-3

Original hardcover edition published in 1985
by Mills & Boon Limited

CHAPTER ONE

'WHAT do you think you're doing?'

Danny looked blankly at the man who had stepped out of the night shadows, sure that above the din she was making she had heard him ask that question. And yet she couldn't have done; it must surely be obvious what she was doing, the lawn-mower moving smoothly in front of her, the sweet smell of newly cut grass fresh in the air.

His appearance in her garden surprised her even more, his wide chest and shoulders bare, the dark hair there disappearing in a vee over the taut stomach and down beneath body-hugging black underwear, his long legs and feet bare too. She had no idea where he had come from and thought she should be the one to be asking that question. She was in her own private garden, mowing her own lawn, and this almost naked man had invaded that privacy.

She suddenly realised how very much alone she was here, her nearest neighbour up at the main house, and as she rarely saw anyone from there since Henry Sutherland had bought the house and grounds and moved in with his entourage she didn't think she would get any help from England's answer to Howard Hughes! Her denim cut-offs and halter-necked yellow top were little covering for her generous curves, and she sought the man's face in the darkness, hoping to read his intent there.

7

What did he look like? What was he thinking? *Who* was he?

'I said——' he repeated, raising his voice.

'I heard what you said,' Danny assured him as she switched off the motor to the mower, wiping her hands down her denim-clad thighs. 'But I think you have that the wrong way around.' She looked at him with eyes that glowed the colour of deep sherry. 'What are *you* doing here?'

The man stepped forward into the light streaming from the lounge window of her cottage behind them, and Danny caught her breath at the raw savage beauty of that harshly lean face. Dark, slightly overlong hair fell forward over his forehead, his eyes a curious light colour, neither blue nor grey, but somewhere in between, his nose a harsh slash, his mouth thinned in a straight line, deep grooves etched beside his nose and mouth. He looked coldly arrogant, and somehow Danny knew he offered no threat to her, that those icy eyes could never deepen with the emotion it would take to physically attack her, that his power was all of the will rather than the body.

'I suppose you do realise it's after eleven o'clock at night?'

Her eyes widened at the question; it had been the last thing she had expected. She was as aware of the time as she was of what she was doing!

'And that mower is damned noisy,' he added hardly at her lack of response.

Her brows knit together. 'What does that have to do with you?'

His mouth thinned. 'It's a still summer's night, the sound carries.'

'Well I—Oh dear.' Contrition darkened the brown glow of her eyes. 'Could it be heard at the main house?' she asked with dread.

'Would you care?' He derided her lack of concern so far in the conversation.

'Well, I wouldn't want to disturb Howard Hughes—sorry, I meant Mr Sutherland.' She blushed at the slip.

'You consider him a recluse?' The man frowned.

Danny shrugged. 'Well, I can't think of any other name for a man who lives behind a ten-foot wall most of the time, has a couple of guard-dogs patrolling the grounds, surrounds himself with numerous bodyguards—can you?' She quirked mischievous brows at him a shade darker than her straight red-gold hair, now secured in a single braid to just below her shoulders.

The man's mouth twisted. 'When you put it that way, no. And to answer your other question, *I* was at the main house when I heard the mower.'

'Oh dear.' She chewed on her bottom lip, her expression suddenly brightening. 'He isn't there, is he?' She grinned her relief. 'I remember I heard the helicopter leave earlier.' She had been most disgusted when part of the grounds of the main house had been taken and turned into a helicopter-pad for the new owner, the comings and goings of the machine a noisy irritant. Old Mrs Prendergast, the previous owner, would turn over in her grave if she knew what they had done to her precious manor house. 'Where's he gone this time?' Danny asked interestedly.

'You have yet to tell me what you're doing mowing the lawn at this ungodly hour.' The man sounded more irritated than ever.

'I always mow the lawn when I'm upset,' she confided. 'I think better then, you see.'

Grey eyes snapped with impatience. 'And couldn't you have done this thinking at a more reasonable time?'

'I didn't know at a more reasonable time that I had something to think about,' she explained. 'I need to think now, and it never used to disturb Mrs Prendergast. Although that could have been because she was as deaf as a post,' she added thoughtfully.

'I see.' The beautifully moulded lips twitched as if in humour, although no smile actually materialised. 'Well, I'm not, and it was disturbing the swim I was taking.'

'Swimming!' she said with some relief. 'You're wearing *swimming trunks*!'

'Well, of course I . . . What did you think I was wearing?' he asked drily. 'No,' he drawled. 'Don't answer that.' He looked over at the cottage. 'Doesn't the mower disturb your grandfather?'

'I hope not.' She looked surprised. 'He's been dead ten years!'

The man looked taken aback. 'But I understood this was the head-gardener's cottage.'

Danny grinned at his perplexity. 'You understood correct.' She nodded.

'Then he's your father?'

'Nope,' she laughed lightly. 'I live here alone.'

'But you can't be Danny Martin.' He shook his head in denial of that fact.

She frowned at his emphatic tone. 'Why can't I?'

'Because I've seen him about the grounds,' the man said tersely. 'He's about seventy years old, with grey hair, and a stooped back!'

'Zacky Boone.' She instantly recognised him by the description. 'And you would have a stooped back, too, if you had been gardening as long as he has!'

'*You're* the head-gardener?' He still didn't look convinced.

'Third generation,' she assured him proudly. 'Dad had no boys, you see, and as I was the oldest girl I was the natural choice to take over from him when he retired.'

'I don't see anything natural about the choice.' His steely gaze raked over her critically. 'Wasn't there something else you would rather have been doing?'

'Wasn't there something else you would rather have been doing than watching over Henry Sutherland?' she instantly came back. 'It can't take a lot of intelligence to be a bodyguard.' She had decided as they spoke that was what he had to be, the height and breadth of him, the muscular physique seeming to imply as much. 'You don't look as if you're just brawn and muscle with nothing up top,' she observed.

'Thank you,' he accepted with dry sarcasm. 'But I can assure you that the bodyguards employed here don't have "nothing up top" either,' he told her grimly. 'They're very intelligent men, with the quick senses to match.'

'Oops.' She grimaced at his anger. 'I didn't mean to step on anyone's toes.'

'You haven't stepped on mine,' he assured her abruptly. 'I don't happen to be a bodyguard.'

'Oh?'

'My name is Sutherland—Pierce Sutherland——'

'Oh God, not another one.' She gave him an angry glare.

Grey-blue eyes clouded with puzzlement. 'I'm sorry?'

'So you should be,' she said crossly.

He looked more confused than ever. 'What have I done?'

'Nothing! But——'

'Thank God for that,' he drawled mockingly.

'But your cousin Nigel has.' She glared at him again. 'At least, I presume he's your cousin.'

The assessing grey-blue eyes swept over her slender body, lingering on the fullness of her breasts before going down to her flat stomach. 'I can't see any evidence of it,' he taunted.

For the first time that she could remember she blushed, she, Danielle Erica Martin, who never blushed. She had chosen to enter a profession consisting mainly of men, had been the only female in her class at college with twenty-five men, and during that time she had become immune to personal remarks and innuendoes; she had had to or walk around with a permanent blush. But this remark, made by a complete stranger, was a little too personal to ignore.

'I didn't mean to me.' She shot Pierce Sutherland a resentful glare. This was serious, damn it. 'He's seducing my sister Cheryl into breaking her engagement to the boy she's been in love with since she was fifteen years old!' she told him indignantly.

Dark brows met over grey-blue eyes. 'Doesn't the lady have to be willing for that?'

'Not when she's faced with a charming, good-looking, intelligent man who seemingly has an unending supply of money at his disposal with which to grant her every wish!'

'Hm,' he murmured. 'I see your point; your sister has become a mercenary.'

'No! Are you sure your name is Sutherland?' She eyed him suspiciously.

This time there was definitely a twitch to the firm lips. 'Which family trait am I lacking in?'

Well, the first she hadn't known him long enough to judge, the second couldn't be doubted, not when he was almost naked not ten feet away from her, the fourth she would take on trust because of his name; it was difficult to tell a person's wealth when their only clothing was a pair of brief swimming trunks! It was the third trait she doubted.

'Cheryl is not a mercenary,' she defended indignantly. 'She's just momentarily infatuated with this Nigel's seeming ability to do exactly what he wants to do.' A mercenary, in fact. She had called her sister that only this evening when Cheryl telephoned to tell her of the feelings she had for Nigel Patrick, the son of Henry Sutherland's sister, and how she was thinking of breaking her engagement to Gary because of him.

Cheryl and Gary had been going out together for almost five years, it would break his heart if Cheryl left him now. It would break Cheryl's, too, when she came to her senses. The best Danny had been able to do was to persuade her sister to wait a little longer before discussing it with Gary. Her sister's ready agreement to the suggestion showed her that Cheryl wasn't as sure about her feelings for Nigel as she pretended to be.

'And what did you decide had to be done about them as you mowed the lawn?'

'At this ungodly hour,' she finished with a grin.

'Exactly,' Pierce drawled.

'Well, I have two options open to me at the moment,' she related thoughtfully. 'I can either let it run its course—which is a bad idea. Or I can try to show Nigel in a bad light, you know two-timing Cheryl or something like that.' She was eager to know his opinion on the latter; he must know his cousin better than she did.

'That isn't a good idea either.' Pierce shook his head mockingly. 'Nigel may be family, and consequently my opinion's slightly biased, but if he's seeing your sister you can be sure she's the only woman he's seeing; he never concentrates on more than one woman at a time.'

'Then how about past scandals?'

'There aren't any.'

'A playboy?'

'He works at least nine hours a day, often six days a week, as the head of accounts for all Sutherland interests; that doesn't leave him a lot of time to do anything!'

'Bad habits?' She was getting desperate now.

Pierce shook his head. 'I don't know of any.'

'There must be something wrong with him!'

she wailed protestingly. 'Everyone has at least one fault.'

'I believe he used to pull little girls' braids as a boy,' Pierce taunted, looking pointedly at Danny's.

'Very funny.' She glared at him.

'What's your fault?' He raised dark brows.

'I talk to strange men who are wearing only bathing trunks at almost twelve o'clock at night!'

For a moment there was only silence, and then he began to laugh, a rich deep sound that was well worth waiting for. 'And mine is that I listen to the problems of the head-gardener who has a body like Raquel Welch at twelve o'clock at night!'

She quirked light auburn brows at him. 'Would you like to rephrase that?'

'Who has the body of Raquel Welch any time of night?'

'Again,' she prompted drily.

'Who has a body like Raquel Welch any time—period?' he said hopefully.

She gave a light tinkling laugh of enjoyment. 'You're learning.'

'Yes,' he acknowledged ruefully. 'How long has your sister known Nigel?'

'About a month or so; she met him down here when she came home from university for the weekend.' Danny frowned as she once again dwelled on the problem of her sister and Nigel Patrick. 'They've been meeting in London regularly since then.'

'And her fiancé?'

'Lives in Bedmont.'

'Ah.'

Ah, indeed. Bedmont was the nearest town to the estate, probably about twelve miles away, but almost a hundred from London. Cheryl and Gary only saw each other alternate weekends because of the expense of travelling, the two of them supposed to be saving up to get married next summer when Cheryl finished at university.

'The problem appears to be distance,' Pierce agreed thoughtfully. 'Your sister is obviously pining for male company, and Nigel is happily providing it. Could the fiancé move to London?'

In theory that might have worked—except for one thing. 'Gary is in the local ambulance service,' she told him despondently. 'He can't get an instant transfer.'

'Hm.' Pierce frowned.

'Cheryl should be ashamed of herself,' Danny said crossly.

'Because he's an ambulanceman, or because she's thinking of breaking their engagement?'

'Both!'

'Can't your parents talk to her? It seems to me it isn't really your problem.'

'When Dad retired last year he and Mum went to Cornwall; I don't want to worry them with this.' She shook her head, loose tendrils of hair about her face.

'Why not, you're worried.' He frowned.

'I'm the eldest . . .'

'How old is that?' he asked sceptically.

'Twenty-one. But——'

'A baby,' he derided. 'And how old is Cheryl?'

'Nineteen. But——'

'Old enough to make her own mistakes—or

not, whatever the case may be,' he dismissed arrogantly.

'I'm a baby, but she isn't?' Danny mocked.

'Touché,' he drawled drily. 'But I still think you should let your sister make the decision without any help from you.'

'She always makes the wrong one and regrets it afterwards.' Danny shook her head. 'Look, I'm sorry I bothered you, this is really not your problem,' she smiled openly, 'I'm sure you want to get back to your swim, and I have to get back to my thinking.'

'But not the lawn-mower, I hope?'

'No,' she laughed. 'Not the lawn-mower. I'm really sorry about that, I just wasn't thinking.'

'I thought you *were* thinking!'

She observed him with her head tilted to one side. 'I think perhaps you are a Sutherland after all.'

His mouth twisted. 'I'll decide whether or not that's a compliment on my walk back to the pool; you certainly don't seem to have a very high opinion of the Sutherlands.'

Danny shook her head. 'I like you.'

'Thank you,' he accepted gravely. 'I hope you can come up with a solution to the Cheryl–Nigel affair.'

'Oh, it isn't an affair,' she quickly defended. 'At least, Cheryl assured me they aren't sleeping together.'

'Does any couple having an affair actually "sleep" together?' Pierce mocked drily.

'I wouldn't know.' She unconsciously revealed her own innocence, although she wouldn't have cared if she had realised; she didn't wear her virginity like a talisman, but neither was she ashamed of it. When the time, and the man, were right, she knew she wouldn't give two thoughts to her virginity. 'I wish you hadn't said that.' She frowned. 'Now I'm really worried.'

'I shouldn't be,' he derided. 'Nigel doesn't actually seduce innocents.'

'Cheryl isn't that innocent.' Danny grimaced, knowing her sister and Gary had been making love for some time.

'Oh.'

'Don't worry, I'll think of something,' she assured Pierce. 'I've been getting Cheryl out of one scrape or another all our lives.'

'Then it's time you had a rest from it.'

'I will.' She nodded. 'Once she's safely married to Gary.'

'I hope you're successful.'

Danny stood and watched him as he opened the wrought-iron gate that separated her small walled cottage from the main immediate grounds, liking the dark thickness of his hair, his wide shoulders, the play of muscles over his back, his tapered waist and narrowed hips, his legs long and muscled, his whole body deeply tanned. The lines of cynicism she had seen on his face, the thread of silver in his dark hair, had indicated that he was probably nearing his fortieth year, and yet he was as lithe as a twenty-year-old. She found herself liking the look of Pierce Sutherland very much.

Suddenly she didn't want to let him go, running across the newly cut lawn to open her gate and follow him as he walked towards the lights of the grey-stoned manor house. 'Hey, Pierce, I——'

'For God's sake!' His expression was fierce as he turned to see her running lightly after him. 'Go back,' he shouted harshly. 'Danny, go back!'

She came to an abrupt halt, staring at him with stricken eyes. Why had he returned to his initial coldness so suddenly? Minutes ago he had . . .

'Danny, go back!' He began to run back to her as the sound of the dogs barking could be heard, all the time the sound coming closer and closer. 'Oh God!' he groaned as the two Alsatians bounded around the corner of the house, still barking as they ran towards them, two of the biggest of their breed Danny had ever seen. 'Heel!' Pierce commanded as he turned to face them, pushing Danny behind him. 'For God's sake heel!' He was breathing hard in his effort to stop the howling beasts.

'*Sit*, you two.' Danny stepped in front of Pierce, the two panting dogs obediently sitting down at her feet, looking up at her with adoring eyes as she patted them affectionately on the head. She turned back to Pierce. 'It's all right, they won't hurt you while you're with me.' She smiled at him reassuringly, concerned at how pale he was.

'I—thought—they—might—attack—you!' he said through gritted teeth.

'Fang and Killer?' She laughed at the thought of them possibly hurting her.

'I believe their names are Ferdinand and Kilpatrick.' He stepped out from behind her, looking down in amazement at the two stupidly drooling dogs that were supposed to be trained killers, Kilpatrick even rolling over on his back now to have his stomach rubbed by one slender, playful hand.

'Oh, they are.' Danny nodded. 'Such silly names for these fearsome creatures.'

'They don't look very fearsome at the moment.' Pierce looked on with disgust as Ferdinand joined his brother by rolling on his back, his big feet waving ridiculously in the air.

'Oh, you mustn't mind them.' Danny straightened, pulling down the ribbed halter-top as it rode up towards her breasts. 'They know me very well.'

'They know me, too,' he derided. 'But they don't "roll over" for me!'

She frowned. 'You seemed frightened of them a moment ago . . .?'

'I told you, I thought they were going to attack you,' he explained impatiently. 'I had no idea they were aware of your scent.'

'We're old friends.' She absently stroked the two regal heads as the dogs stood as close to her as they could get. 'Danton introduced me to them their first day here; he thought it best in the circumstances.'

'Yes,' he agreed tersely. 'Speaking of Danton,' his eyes narrowed as he looked about them, 'he should have been here with his dogs by now.'

Danny shook her head. 'He probably thinks they're taking a run with me, we usually take one together late at night when it isn't so hot. I just haven't had the time tonight.'

Grey eyes were disbelieving. 'You run Danton's dogs for him?'

'Of course not,' she scorned. 'They just run along with me when I jog five times around the wall perimeter.'

'Good God, how far is that?'

'About five miles, I think. Then I——'

'Don't tell me any more!' He closed his eyes. 'What on earth do you want to half kill yourself in that way every night for?'

'I don't half kill myself.' She smiled at his horror. 'I'm keeping myself in shape—my Raquel Welch shape,' she added teasingly.

'Gardening doesn't do that?'

Danny shook her head. 'It doesn't loosen up the muscles like jogging does.'

'But it doesn't kill you either!'

'Exercise, properly supervised, doesn't harm you at all,' she reproved. 'I'm sure you don't keep your own body in that great shape by sitting about all day.' The candidness of her gaze showed him just how good she thought that body was.

'I swim thirty lengths of the pool daily,' he grudgingly admitted.

'There you are, then,' she said smugly. 'Actually, that's why I came after you.'

'Because of my great body?' he lightly mocked.

'I think you're learning a little too fast now.' She pretended irritation, the twinkle in her sherry-coloured eyes belying that emotion. 'I wondered if I could join you in your swim.'

'You can think in a pool, too?'

'I've never tried.' She shrugged. 'I didn't really have that in mind when I suggested the swim.'

'Oh?'

'My, what a suspicious mind you have, Mr Sutherland.' Danny looked up at him reprovingly. 'Your uncle lives in a sterilely safe world but I would have thought you had more sense. I certainly don't have designs on that great body of yours,' she said angrily.

He had stiffened at the mention of his reclusive uncle, but his expression lightened at the latter, until finally he smiled, albeit resignedly. 'Go and get your bikini, Danny,' he sighed. 'I'd hate you to miss your daily exercise and lose that figure.'

An imp of mischief possessed her as she looked for her bathing costume, picking up one of Cheryl's, a skimpy black article on her petite sister, even more so on her more generous curves. But Pierce's last comment had been a little patronising, and she intended shaking him out of his arrogant complacency.

She certainly did that when she joined him, waiting until he surfaced at the side of the pool before dropping her black robe, almost giggling out loud at the widening of Pierce's eyes as he leant his chin on his folded arms, water dripping down his face.

'I was wrong,' he said slowly. 'Your body is better than Raquel Welch's!'

She moved to the poolside with exaggeratedly provocative movements. 'Eat your heart out, Pierce Sutherland.' She gave him a sweetly triumphant smile. 'I've already promised not to touch you.'

He watched her as she slowly entered the water by the stairs. 'I didn't make the same promise,' he reminded huskily. 'Although we would have little privacy here.' He grimaced.

She glanced up at the brightly lit windows. The pool, another recent addition for the new owner, was built close to the back of the three-storey house. 'Mr Sutherland isn't back in the house, is he?' she prompted cautiously, doubting Henry Sutherland would like the idea of his gardener cavorting about in his pool with his nephew.

Pierce shook his head. 'I can assure you Henry is not in the house.'

'Do you call him that?' She swam over to his side, treading water when she reached him. 'It doesn't seem respectful somehow. He's a very powerful man, isn't he?' She wrinkled her nose at one man having as much power as Henry Sutherland was reputed to have.

'Very,' Pierce agreed grimly.

'Where do you fit into the scheme of things?' she asked interestedly. 'Your cousin does the accounts,' she explained at his questioning look. 'I wondered what you did for the Sutherland empire.'

'A bit of this, a bit of that.' Pierce shrugged dismissively. 'It's a big organisation.'

She nodded, looking appreciatively at the blue-bottomed pool, liking the privacy the fenced-in area offered—except from the house itself! 'How many lengths have you done?'

'Ten.' He shook the water from his hair. 'Feel up to doing the other twenty?'

'I can try.' She nodded. 'Although don't make it a race; I'm completely out of practice. They closed the pool down in Bedmont, you know,' she told him as they struck out in leisurely strokes.

Pierce moved smoothly through the water, obviously pacing himself to her slower movements. 'Feel free to use this one any time you want.'

'Won't your uncle mind the intrusion?'

'Henry can be a very generous person,' he told her drily.

'I suppose it's nice for him, having his two nephews working for him,' she said thoughtfully. 'He doesn't have any children of his own, does he?'

'No.'

'I heard his wife died.'

'A long time ago,' Pierce confirmed abruptly.

'How sad. And he never married again?'

'No.'

'It seems a pity, I'm sure he must have a lot to give a relationship.'

Pierce's mouth twisted. 'He is very rich.'

'I didn't mean in that way.' She gave him a stern look for his cynicism. 'With all that wealth he must also be a very travelled man. Very interesting, I should think.'

'To my knowledge no woman has ever wanted him for his mind,' Pierce drawled drily.

Amusement flickered in warm brown eyes. 'Now *that* is disrespectful,' she teased.

'But true,' he rasped, striking out in stronger movements. 'Let's speed this up or we'll be here all night!'

She managed fifteen lengths before hauling herself out and collapsing on the cool marble surround to the pool. By the time she had recovered her breath enough to sit up Pierce was on his final length. He glided easily through the water, obviously not tiring at all, his strokes still strong and smooth, a grim look of satisfaction to his face as he levered out on to the side, picking up a towel to drape it around his neck.

'I've been thinking . . .'

'Well, it worked for one of us, didn't it.' She grinned.

His brows rose. 'You have no solution to your problem?'

'Not yet, but I'll find one,' she dismissed confidently. 'You were thinking . . .?'

'When you go on this late night jog of yours,' he dropped down on to the marble beside her, 'why don't alarms go off and the lights come on?'

'It's quite a security system, isn't it,' she acknowledged. 'What does your uncle have in the house that he needs to protect?'

Pierce's mouth twisted. 'That most elusive possession, privacy.'

Danny grimaced. 'And an expensive one, too, if the guards and security system are anything to go by.'

'You didn't answer my question,' he prompted hardly.

'About the bells and lights?' She shrugged. 'Dave Benson switches them off while I take my run.'

'He *what*?'

Danny frowned at his harsh anger. 'Don't panic,' she teased. 'There's still the visual surveillance, and the actual guards. Besides, it isn't for very long, and——'

'Long enough,' Pierce ground out fiercely, his

eyes icy grey. 'I can't believe this.' He shook his
head. 'Are you really telling me that Benson
switches off a million pounds worth of highly
technical equipment so that you can jog five miles
a night?'

'A million pounds?' Danny gasped at the
figure. 'Is that really how much it cost? I know
he's a rich man, but——'

'*Does he?*'

She shrugged. 'I don't know what all the fuss is
about, it's only for a few minutes——'

'Long enough for someone to get in to the
grounds and up to the house,' Pierce snapped,
anger etched deeply into his face.

She shook her head. 'Not with the dogs loose.'

'Ferdinand and Kilpatrick are with you,
remember,' he bit out tersely.

Danny gave an impatient sigh. 'In that case
there are still the men patrolling the house and
immediate grounds.'

'After learning of the shambles you've made of
the rest of the security system I wouldn't be
surprised to know that they're watching you, too!
God,' he exploded into a sitting position. 'This is
incredible!'

She chewed on her bottom lip as she realised
how seriously upset he was. 'Are you going to tell
your uncle?' She grimaced.

His head snapped round, his breathing uneven.
'You can be sure he needs to be told what's going
on in his own house!' he told her hardily.

'What will he do?'

'Well, I wouldn't advise any more late night
trips into the grounds,' he warned grimly.

'Dave Benson isn't going to get into trouble, is he?' she asked pleadingly, wishing she had just kept her mouth shut. But it had been something she had never been able to do. Besides, she hadn't realised it would cause this fuss.

'Mr Benson is going to get exactly what he deserves!'

His steely tone made her cringe. Pierce Sutherland was obviously a man without mercy, which led her to wonder if he wasn't his uncle's hatchet-man; he gave the impression of having to make harsh decisions and seeing that they were carried out.

'Pierce, I——'

'What do you think you're doing?' he rasped, looking down at her coldly.

Sherry-coloured eyes widened in bewilderment. 'Sorry?'

He looked down pointedly at the hand she had placed on his chest as she made her plea.

Danny looked down at the hand too, the skin almost the same colour as his own mahogany, hours spent working in the grounds meaning it wasn't a pretty or delicate hand, the nails were kept short and square, the long fingers were capable rather than refined, several callouses on her palm. No, it wasn't a pretty hand, but it didn't deserve the dissecting regard Pierce was giving it, either.

'Why are you touching me?' he asked slowly.

She breathed softly as she realised the reason for his terse query. 'I talk with my hands,' she dismissed. 'My father says that if my hands were tied behind my back I'd be silent.'

'I doubt that,' Pierce drawled derisively.

'It's true. I——' The light explanation was cut off as firmly moulded lips descended almost roughly on to her own.

Surprise was quickly followed by pleasure, and with a low groan of surrender she curved her body in to his, her arms going up about his neck, opening her lips as the rigidity of his tongue probed against them.

Her mouth widened even more as she gasped at the coolness of the marble against her back as she was lowered to the ground, the hardness of Pierce's chest crushing her breasts in a most erotic way, the peaks erect through her bikini top.

'Danny—— What *is* your name?' Pierce demanded against the curve of her breast.

She mumbled her reply, surprised she could *remember* her name, feeling dizzy at the expertise of this man's kisses. God, he . . .

'I'm sorry, Mr Sutherland, I had no idea——! My God, Danny!' Don Bridgeman, Head of Security for the Sutherland estate, gasped as he stood several feet away from them, his dark-suited figure strangely out of place.

'What is it?' Pierce sat up, effectively shielding Danny as she straightened her bikini.

'We have a security alert on the west wall——'

'I'm surprised you were aware of it,' Pierce snapped with icy reproval as he stood up.

'Sir . . .?' Don Bridgeman looked puzzled.

'Never mind,' Pierce dismissed. 'I'll talk to you about that later. Wait for me outside.'

Danny watched the exchange with a puzzled frown, feeling sorry for the older man, knowing his rebuke had all been her fault. But how was she supposed to know her casually given admission would cause this much trouble; the alarm was only off for a matter of minutes, for goodness' sake!

'I'm sorry about this.' Pierce put out a hand to pull her to her feet, instantly releasing her as she straightened. 'I had no idea we would be interrupted.'

She dismissed the apology with an impatient shrug. 'What are you going to do about Dave Benson?'

His head went back haughtily. 'I don't believe that is any of your business.'

'But——'

'If you'll excuse me, I have to go and check on this break in security,' he cut in pointedly.

Danny would have liked to have said more, but she could see by the implacability of his rigidly clenched jaw that Pierce wasn't in the mood to listen. With a shrug she collected up her robe and left, the mischievous leaps and bounds of Ferdinand and Kilpatrick as they accompanied her back to the cottage not soothing her at all. Pierce seemed to be a powerful and respected man—and she was more deeply attracted to him than any man she had ever met.

CHAPTER TWO

'ANY more lemon meringue pie?'

Danny stood up with a smile, going to the dish that stood on top of the cooker.

'You make the best lemon meringue pie I've ever tasted.' Gary watched her movements.

It had been a successful meal, plain English cooking, soup, roast beef with all the trimmings, and Gary's favourite dessert, lemon meringue pie, but she knew that was the sort of food he preferred, not a man to go in for exotic food. Thank goodness, because she couldn't cook exotic food!

She had finally come up with this idea midweek, inviting Gary over for a meal, knowing he would mention it to Cheryl the next time he saw her, and knowing that her sister would instantly be suspicious; her lack of cooking ability had become a family joke over the years, and it was something she avoided at all costs. Close as the sisters were, Cheryl would not appreciate Danny inviting Gary here when she herself wasn't present.

Gary was her own age, the two of them in the same class at school, in fact it had been because of their casual friendship that Cheryl and Gary had met and fallen in love. Cheryl would not be pleased to know Gary had spent the evening with Danny.

The idea had come to her as she spent the

afternoon in the seclusion of the vegetable garden, trying desperately to think of some way to bring Cheryl to her senses, her sister having telephoned her again the previous evening before going out to a party with Nigel Patrick. It had suddenly seemed imperative that she do something to stop the relationship, sure that Cheryl would regret it if Gary should find out about the other man. She had decided that a little healthy jealousy on Cheryl's part might not be a bad thing.

Not that Gary saw any romantic interest in her invitation! It would have been insulting if she weren't used to it. Gary never saw any other woman but Cheryl, and so looked on Danny as a sister; he already had two, one more made no difference! He accepted the invitation to dinner because she was Cheryl's sister, had talked of nothing but Cheryl since he arrived. Tall and firmly muscled, his only other real interest besides Cheryl was food, he ate the meal she had prepared in appreciative silence.

'Will Cheryl be coming home this weekend?' she asked as she gave him his third helping of pie. Her sister had been very non-committal about her plans when they spoke two days ago.

'No.' He ate his pie with relish.

She frowned. 'But I thought it was her turn to come home this weekend?'

'It is.' He nodded, his dark hair kept short, his deep blue eyes warm and open, very good-looking in a youthful way. 'But she needs to study,' he dismissed. 'She has her exams soon.'

Danny held back her impatience with effort; the only thing Cheryl would be studying this weekend was Nigel Patrick, she was sure of it. God, her sister was a fool! Not that Nigel Patrick wasn't charming, he was, very, but he was only interested in having a good time, couldn't possibly have any lasting interest in a young girl destined to become an English teacher. Sometimes her sister could be so *stupid*!

'Coffee?' she asked Gary absently, receiving a frowning look as she almost removed his bowl before all the pie had been eaten.

'Thanks.' He sat back, obviously replete. 'Shall I help you clear away here?'

She almost laughed at his lack of enthusiasm for the idea, ushering him into the lounge while she made the coffee. Gary was a typical male, he didn't mind eating the meal, but clearing away the debris was something else entirely. Not that she minded in this case, Gary was something of a menace in the kitchen, usually managing to break at least one thing.

She checked on him while she was waiting for the coffee to percolate, finding him engrossed in the boxing match on the television. No wonder Cheryl found Nigel Patrick more exciting!

She had the coffee ready on a tray when the knock sounded on the back door, and went to answer it. She hadn't seen Pierce Sutherland over the last three days, and she couldn't pretend she wasn't surprised to see him now. For one thing, he looked completely different in the iron-grey pin-striped suit and pale grey shirt, his hair trimmed to a neater style, too. For another thing she just hadn't expected to see him again, their parting the other evening certainly hadn't led her to believe they would.

'I know it's late,' he began in that husky voice.

'It's only ten-thirty,' she mocked.

His mouth twisted. 'I forgot, you're a night-owl. Solved your problem?'

She thought of Gary sitting comfortably replete in the other room. 'Working on it.' She nodded. 'Was everything all right the other night?'

'The security alert?' He nodded. 'Just a malfunction in the system.'

'Would you like to come in?' She belatedly remembered her manners. 'I've just made some coffee.'

'I'll come in,' he accepted. 'But I never drink coffee.'

'Caffeine.' She nodded, closing the door behind him.

'No,' he derided. 'I just don't like it.'

'Oh,' she smiled. 'Tea, then?'

'Nothing, thanks,' he refused abruptly, his height making her cosy kitchen look even smaller.

'Then what can I do for you?' She looked up at him curiously.

'I——'

'Hey, Danny, I— Oh.' Gary came to a confused halt in the doorway, meeting the other man's narrow-eyed gaze with curiosity. 'I didn't realise you had company.' He turned enquiringly to Danny.

'That makes two of us,' Pierce Sutherland put in icily. 'It would seem I've called at an inopportune time,' he added harshly.

'Not at all,' she dismissed easily. 'Gary and I have finished our meal, and . . .'

'Gary?' Pierce echoed slowly.

Danny nodded. 'You remember, I told you about my sister's fiancé.'

'I remember,' he rasped grimly. 'Your method of solving the problem is—unique, Danielle.'

The foreign inflection he gave to her full name was very pleasant, but she couldn't imagine what he thought was so unique about the idea of making her sister jealous. Inspired, perhaps, but certainly not unique.

'I'll leave the two of you to enjoy your coffee,' he added coldly.

'But you didn't tell me why you came over.' She frowned.

'It wasn't important.' He turned to the younger man. 'Sorry to have interrupted your evening.'

'Pierce . . .' She stood in the doorway and watched as he strode off into the darkness, the barking of the dogs silenced by a single word from him tonight. He was a strange man, a very strange man. Almost as strange as his uncle was reputed to be.

'Who was *that*?' Gary was naturally mystified by her visitor.

She closed the door with a sigh. She hadn't expected to see Pierce Sutherland again, knowing that the kiss they had shared hadn't meant the same to him as it had to her. But now that she had seen him again she hated the fact that he had left without telling her why he had come here in the first place.

'He works for Henry Sutherland.' She was

reluctant to mention either of the nephews to Gary, knew he could be very astute when he chose to be.

'Are you and he—friends?' Gary probed.

'No,' she answered truthfully, doubting Pierce Sutherland had many friends, male or female.

'He didn't seem too pleased about seeing me here.' Gary frowned.

'You're imagining things,' she dismissed briskly. 'Now, how about that coffee?'

'That's what I came in to tell you,' he said ruefully. 'Don't bother about coffee for me, I'd better be going; I have an early shift tomorrow.'

The coffee was already made, but she didn't try to dissuade him. Gary was a very nice man, but she had done what she set out to do, and now she didn't mind being left on her own.

She walked down to the gate that divided her garden from the main one after Gary had left, looking over at the main house. The lights around the pool were on, and she could imagine that sleek body moving through the cool water, wishing she could join him. But things had changed in the last three days, no longer was she allowed to enter the grounds at night, the alarms left on now by strict instructions of Henry Sutherland. And poor Dave Benson was under sentence of serious reprimand when Henry Sutherland got back from his latest business trip. She had tried to get in to see the elusive billionaire before he left, intending to plead on Dave's behalf, but she had been firmly told that Mr Sutherland wasn't seeing anyone.

She couldn't blame Pierce for advising his

uncle to take some form of action over the incident, but she didn't feel Dave Benson should be made to take all the blame.

She had heard the helicopter return earlier this evening, and Pierce's presence indicated that his uncle was back in residence, but the lateness of the hour meant she would have to wait until tomorrow before seeing Henry Sutherland. She wished she knew why Pierce had come over . . .

'What are you up to?' Cheryl demanded suspiciously.

The expected telephone call from her sister came early the next evening, Cheryl sounding most indignant. 'Sorry?' She pretended ignorance, holding back her humour.

'Gary said he came to dinner last night,' Cheryl accused.

'He did,' she acknowledged. 'He looks as if he's losing weight to me,' she added lightly. 'I thought a home-cooked meal would be nice.'

'Not one of your home cooked meals!' Cheryl mocked scornfully.

'Gary didn't have any complaints,' she taunted.

'He gets a home-cooked meal every night—he lives at home with his parents!'

'So he does,' she smiled. 'Then something else must be bothering him.'

'I suppose you're implying that it's me,' Cheryl said in a disgruntled voice.

'You?' She feigned surprise. 'Why should Gary be worried about you?'

'Because of Nigel!'

'Oh, but he doesn't know about him,' Danny

dismissed. 'And even if he did, he may not be too worried. You've been away a long time, Cheryl,' she reasoned. 'Men tend to find themselves other—compensations for an absent fiancée.'

'What are you implying now?' her sister demanded waspishly. 'That Gary has someone else?'

'Why not? You do.'

'That's different——'

'I don't see how,' she mocked. 'Gary is very handsome, he has a steady job, a lot of women would be glad to snap him up.'

'He's engaged to me!'

'Engagements don't seem to mean the same as they used to,' she derided.

'Do you know something I don't?' Cheryl asked sharply. 'Has Gary been seeing someone else?'

'Would it really bother you that much if he were?'

'Of course it would!'

'Why? I thought you were thinking of finishing with him anyway,' Danny reasoned.

'I am, but ... Who is it, Danny?' she demanded to know. 'Who is Gary seeing?'

'No one, as far as I know,' Danny answered evasively.

'But you said——' Cheryl broke off, the workings of her mind almost audible over the telephone. 'How late did he stay last night?' she finally asked guardedly.

'Quite late,' Danny prevaricated. 'He can be a very interesting conversationalist.'

'Are you going to invite him over again?'

'I was thinking of asking him tomorrow,' she invented, having hoped the once would be enough to irk her sister.

'You can't,' Cheryl told her with obvious relief. 'He's coming up to London for the weekend.'

'But I thought he was working.' She was genuinely surprised.

'He's managed to change weekends with someone else,' her sister said triumphantly.

'What about Nigel?'

Cheryl sighed. 'He's had to go away un-expectedly,' she grumbled. 'To Germany this time.'

She had known Henry Sutherland was once more away, her efforts to see him earlier today once again met with refusal, but she hadn't thought of Nigel going with him. This wasn't the ideal way she would have wanted Cheryl to be with Gary, but at least they would be together; it was better than nothing. And she knew it had given her sister a jolt to know she had had Gary over for dinner. She could only do so much to keep them together, the rest was up to them.

'I don't—I'll have to go,' she said quickly as a loud knock sounded on the door. 'Someone is at the door.'

'About Gary . . .'

'He's your problem,' she dismissed impatiently, wondering if her visitor could be Pierce; she hoped so. 'But if he didn't refuse dinner with me I doubt he would turn down any other invitations he receives either. It's lonely for him here, Cheryl, I hope you realise that.'

'It's lonely for me too.'

'But you've found someone else to ease your

loneliness,' she reminded. 'So why shouldn't Gary do the same?'

'He wouldn't.'

'I hope you're right.' Danny sighed at her sister's confidence, sadly afraid Cheryl could be right. 'Have a nice weekend, Cheryl, but try to remember that you will have to make a decision between Gary and Nigel soon. I'll call you Monday or Tuesday.' She rang off quickly before her visitor decided she wasn't at home and went away again, her face glowing with pleasure when she opened the door to find Pierce standing there. 'I hoped you would come back tonight.' She pulled him inside. 'You left so suddenly last night.' She beamed up at him.

He seemed slightly dazed by the warmth of his welcome. 'You had company.' He shrugged.

'Only Gary,' Danny dismissed lightly. 'You don't travel with your uncle?'

He frowned, the grey-blue eyes suddenly wary. 'Sorry?'

'I was talking to Cheryl on the telephone when you knocked,' she explained, liking the way the black trousers fitted the lean length of his legs, the grey shirt obviously silk. She felt a bit untidy in her green shorts and lime-green T-shirt, having intended to shower and change after her salad dinner; Cheryl's call had delayed that. 'She was bemoaning the fact that Nigel has gone away to Germany with your uncle.'

'Did he actually tell her that?' Pierce asked slowly.

'Oh God.' She grimaced. 'I haven't found another security malfunction?'

Pierce gave a half smile, at once looking less severe and remote. 'Not that I'm aware,' he drawled. 'But Henry Sutherland certainly isn't going to be anywhere near Germany this weekend.'

Danny gave him a startled look. 'Are you sure?'

'He arrived home late this afternoon, and as far as I know he intends staying here for several days.'

She chewed on her bottom lip. 'Then I wonder why Nigel told Cheryl that?' She frowned. 'Let's go through to the lounge and make ourselves comfortable,' she suggested absently, moving with her usual grace, sitting cross-legged on the sofa. 'Please, sit down,' she invited as Pierce hesitated in the low doorway, the beams on the ceiling almost touching his head as he crossed the room. 'Mind!' she warned as he almost walked into the light hanging from the middle of the ceiling.

'An original cottage, I presume,' he said drily. 'Like the house.'

'Wonderful, aren't they,' Danny acknowledged admiringly. 'We've decorated the cottage since my grandfather lived here, of course . . .'

'Obviously,' Pierce mocked.

She gave an appreciative chuckle. 'But otherwise we've tried to keep it the same. It's very cosy in the winter with the fire burning.'

'I'm sure. Only Gary?' he prompted softly.

Danny frowned at the sudden change of subject. 'Gary Cartwright? Cheryl's fiancé?'

'Yes, your sister's fiancé,' Pierce acknowledged with steel in his voice. 'When I said you had company last night you replied "Only Gary".

I take it that young man was your sister's fiancé?'

Young man? He made Gary sound in a different generation, and as she was Gary's contemporary . . . she wouldn't have that! 'Yes, that was Gary,' she confirmed. 'He left just after you did, he has to be up early for work in the mornings. Why do you suppose Nigel lied to Cheryl?'

'Why do you?'

'I thought you said he only concentrated on one woman at a time,' she reminded.

He shrugged broad shoulders, a certain tension about him even though he seemed relaxed in the chair he had chosen to sit in. Danny wondered if he ever completely relaxed. 'Perhaps I don't know him as well as I thought I did,' he drawled. 'Will you tell your sister?'

She shook her head. 'She would just think I'm being vindictive. Letting her think I have designs on Gary is a much better idea.'

Grey eyes blinked, his face remaining expressionless. 'Is that what you were doing last night?'

She nodded. 'I like Gary, and I think Cheryl is treating him very badly.'

'I see.'

'No, you don't,' she laughed at his disapproving look. 'Gary sees me as another sister; he already has two. And he's been in our family circle for so long that I think of him as a brother in return. You still haven't told me why you came over last night.'

'I wanted to explain to you why such action has been taken over the security man called Benson.'

'Oh, I understand that it was wrong to turn off the alarms.' She sobered. 'He does, too——'

'I should damn well hope so!'

'But he still kept up the visual surveillance,' she added protestingly.

'It wasn't enough.'

'Pierce——'

'Danielle, it was Benson's responsibility to take care of night security,' he cut in grimly, his mouth tight. 'As an ex-policeman he should have known better.'

'Why do you do that?' she asked curiously.

'Benson is——'

'No, not that—although we'll get back to him in a moment. No one else calls me Danielle.'

'Danny makes you sound like a man.' He scowled.

'As you once thought me.' She nodded. 'Oh, don't worry, I'm not complaining. It makes me feel special.'

Grey eyes looked at her probingly. 'Why should you want that, Danielle?' he asked softly.

'Why not?' She looked at him with candid brown eyes. 'You don't have a girl in every country like your cousin seems to, do you?'

The forbidding mouth quirked mockingly. 'I don't have a girl—or preferably, woman, in any country,' Pierce derided.

'No?' She found that a little hard to believe, sensing that beneath the reserved coldness was a man of deep passion. Hadn't she tasted a little of that passion the other night? Didn't she want to taste it again!

'No,' he spoke harshly now.

'Would you like one,' she encouraged hopefully. 'In England, that is?'

His mouth tightened even more. 'Are you offering your services?'

Perhaps it was the way he said 'services', or maybe it was just his tone of voice, but she found the words slightly insulting. 'I'd like to get to know you better,' she answered with a frown. 'I'd also like to go swimming again,' she added lightly.

'Another mercenary,' Pierce taunted.

'Not me.' She shook her head. 'I just felt that as you're partly responsible for my late night jogging being curtailed you wouldn't mind offering the use of the pool for my excercise instead.'

'I told you before,' he rasped, 'you're free to use it at any time.'

'You're sure it won't disturb your uncle?' She frowned.

'Yes.'

'Have you had your swim today yet?'

'That isn't very subtle, Danielle,' he drawled, his eyes mocking.

'Do I have to be?' she complained. 'I've never been one to indulge in those pointless guessing games. I'd like us to become friends, and as you don't seem to be around too often I have to take advantage of the opportunities I do have.'

His brows rose in some surprise. 'You're certainly different from the women I usually meet.'

'Have there been a lot of them?'

'The mere fact that I consider you too young for me to answer that question tells me this conversation shouldn't be taking place at all,' he bit out.

'But it is.'

He made an impatient sound in his throat. 'Woman have never figured that strongly in my life,' he answered distantly, as if he weren't used to people delving so closely into his private life. 'When I want one I take one, it's as simple as that.'

Danny gave an inward wince at his candidness, as he had probably guessed that she would. But she freely acknowledged that he had been brought up in, and inhabited, a completely different world from her own, one where real emotions were hard to find, his very name making him a target for women and so increasing his cynicism where they were concerned. It couldn't be easy being a Sutherland, even if he was just a nephew to Henry Sutherland.

'And do you—take one—often?' She looked at him with widely innocent eyes.

'If you're trying to ascertain how highly sexed I am let me assure you that my appetite is that of the average male. I am in no desperate need of a woman right now,' he dismissed coldly. 'And when I am I choose women who will not be a problem to me afterwards.'

She had only asked the question in the hope of repaying some of the shock-value he had given out; it had backfired on her! 'Very sensible.' She unbent her long legs to stand up. 'Shall we have that swim now?'

'Danielle——'

'Yes?' She looked at him with calm brown eyes.

'Nothing,' he dismissed impatiently, also

standing up, the small room suddenly seeming even smaller. 'Please use the pool,' he invited abruptly. 'I don't have the time to join you.'

'Oh.' She was too disappointed not to show it.

He gave a impatient sigh. 'Danielle, has no one ever told you it's dangerous to show this much——'

'Enthusiasm?' she finished lightly. 'I've always been the same, I don't see any reason to change now.'

'And where do you think it will get you?' Pierce asked softly.

When she looked into those icy grey eyes she didn't think it would get her anywhere, not with this man, at least. Her candidness was obviously not welcome. 'At this moment? Into the pool, I hope.' Her eyes gleamed with mischief as she saw his sudden expulsion of air.

Some of the tension seemed to leave the broad shoulders, too. 'Then I won't keep you from it any longer,' he told her distantly.

'Pierce . . .?'

'Yes?' He was wary again.

Danny wished she knew what made him act that way, it made her feel uncomfortable. 'You said your uncle is at home tonight?'

His eyes narrowed. 'Yes.'

'Do you think I might be able to see him?'

'Well certainly not this evening——'

'Tomorrow,' she corrected laughingly. 'Do you think I could see him then? I've been trying the last few days, but he's been away.'

'What's it about?'

'Dave Benson.'

Pierce's mouth tightened. 'I've already told you that he has to take responsibility for the lapse,' he bit out harshly. 'Appealing on his behalf won't do any good.'

She shrugged. 'Nevertheless, I'd still like to speak to your uncle.'

He nodded, as if he had never doubted her determination. 'Come over to the house tomorrow afternoon.'

'He won't mind?' She frowned at his freely given invitation after she had had so much trouble seeing him so far.

Pierce's mouth twisted. 'He never minds seeing a beautiful woman.'

Her eyes widened with surprise. 'How old is your uncle?' She had assumed he would be well into his fifties.

'Not too old to appreciate a beautiful woman; no man is ever *that* old!'

'Am I beautiful?'

He gave a husky chuckle, looking younger, lines etched beside his eyes and mouth. 'You would make a very good businesswoman, Danielle; you don't miss the slightest slip.'

She shook her head, answering seriously. 'Shrubs and flowers are much easier to understand than people, especially the sharks of the business world.'

'You don't seem to have had too much trouble with me,' he drawled.

'Oh, I didn't mean——'

'I know,' he mocked. 'I'll tell Benson you'll be over shortly,' he added briskly. 'I don't suppose there's any need to warn you about the ferocious guard-dogs patrolling the grounds!'

She smiled at his derisive sarcasm. 'You should have seen the look on your face when Fang and Killer ran towards us!' She began to giggle, reliving the moment. 'I wish I'd had a camera!'

'I'm glad you didn't,' he said with self-disgust. 'I can assure you I don't usually make such a fool of myself.'

No, she could tell he was very uncomfortable with the fact that he might have looked remotely silly. He was a man who was ultimately in control of any situation, had a dignity that didn't allow for errors, a sense of self-preservation that didn't allow others to make them either. Which brought her back to Dave Benson.

'I'll come over to the house at two-thirty tomorrow afternoon,' she told Pierce.

He shook his head. 'It won't do any good. The man is on a month's notice.'

'I didn't know that,' she gasped her dismay.

Grey eyes narrowed to steely slits. 'What did you think had happened to him?'

'He told me he had received a reprimand——'

'For what he did he should have received an instant dismissal!'

'Then it's lucky your uncle is a more reasonable man than you appear to be, isn't it!' she flashed. 'Honestly, Pierce, how can you be so bloody-minded?' she said impatiently. 'Dave Benson is a good man. Good gracious, I'm as much to blame as he is!'

'Perhaps you would like to be dismissed, too?' he arched dark brows at her. 'I'm sure it could be arranged,' he added icily.

In control—this man was unreasonable! 'Surely that's for your uncle to decide?' she challenged, her head back, her eyes glittering defiantly.

'Not necessarily,' he said dangerously soft.

'I think you've been shut in behind these ten-foot walls too long,' she snapped. 'Your judgement seems to have become warped; you've lost touch with the real world!'

'I know the real world very well, Danielle,' he rasped harshly. 'Much better than you, if you did but know it!'

She shook her head. 'I still like and trust people, Pierce; do you?'

He looked dangerous as his mouth tightened ominously. 'Certain members of my family I like—although not all. And I trust no one.'

'How sad for you,' she said instantly.

'Not at all,' he drawled. 'It makes life a lot easier.'

'But lonelier.'

'Loneliness is a condition of the mind, not the body. You can be alone in a room full of people, just as you can be completely fulfilled in a room on your own.'

'Ah, but which is preferable?'

'For me? The latter. For you it's obviously the former,' he added mockingly.

'Don't presume that you know me just because I'm basically a forthright person,' Danny bit out curtly. 'I have as many complexities as the next person! Maybe not as many as you,' she added bitchily. 'But then I think that would be quite difficult!'

His mouth quirked with amusement. 'You have a temper I would never have guessed at,' he drawled. 'I presume that can be attributed to the red in your hair.'

'It can be attributed to the fact that you make too *many* presumptions.' She glared at him.

'Has anyone ever told you that you're beautiful when you're angry?' he taunted.

'I don't know anyone that corny!'

His amusement deepened as he took her in his arms, stilling her struggles by pinning her arms at her sides. 'I'll admit my verbal technique may be a little hackneyed,' he murmured softly, 'but my physical one isn't!'

She soon found that out, the kisses they had shared the other evening nothing compared to this onslaught. Pierce crushed her to him, bending her to his will, his mouth plundering and possessing her own until she could only cling to him.

Her arms crept up about his neck as she raised up to meet the fire of Pierce's lips, her breasts pressed into the hardness of his chest, the nipples aching and hard. They didn't ache for long as Pierce pushed her T-shirt up her body, bending his head to suckle at each throbbing tip, the tugging caress causing a languid ache between her thighs, an ache that he caressed with the palm of his hand, the circular motions bringing moist heat to her body.

'Pierce . . .?'

He raised his head to look down at her with glazed eyes. 'I could lay you down on this carpet and take you right now!' he scorned harshly, his mouth twisting as she made no denial. 'But I'm not going to.' He pushed her away from him, pulling her T-shirt down over the heavy weight of her breasts. 'I haven't lost touch with *that* reality!'

Danny turned away, her arms wrapped protectively about her waist. 'I've changed my mind about the swim,' she told him hollowly. 'If you could just tell your uncle I'd like to see him.'

He gave a heavy sigh. 'Danielle . . .'

'Do you always leave your women feeling this empty?' she asked dully.

'*What?*'

'Your technique *is* good, Pierce.' She turned to face him. 'But when that's all it is it's apt to leave the recipient feeling in a vacuum.' If the truth were known she felt a victim of her own attraction for this man. Because she did still find him attractive, she just didn't understand him, doubted if anyone did. 'Maybe it's all to do with the fact that you don't like people, even women.' She shook her head. 'I feel sorry for you.'

'Don't,' he scorned mockingly. 'I can always pay a woman to like me.'

'But do you like them?'

'Does that really matter?'

She had been wrong about this man, he didn't *want* to find real emotions, preferred to pay for false ones. He was a man who was simply beyond her comprehension. 'Obviously not,' she said flatly, numbed by such coldness.

'Definitely not,' he derided. 'Henry will expect you tomorrow,' he told her abruptly before leaving, the faint aroma of his aftershave left elusively in the air.

*   *   *

The house had been completely redecorated and refurnished since Mrs Prendergast died and the estate had been sold to Henry Sutherland. Gone were the faded, slightly fraying carpets, and the worn furniture, and in their place were thick deep-pile carpets and Persian rugs, the furniture still antique, but in excellent condition, the decor mellow and relaxing. It had always been a beautiful house, now it looked magnificent.

Danny hadn't actually been inside it since Henry Sutherland took over and made the changes, and it was good to see that they had been improvements; she still wasn't too sure about the helicopter-pad and swimming-pool outside.

Dave Benson had escorted her over to the house, asking her not to go through with talking to Henry Sutherland, that their employer had a perfect right to dismiss him, that he had acted like a damn fool. But Danny was well aware that if it hadn't been for her he wouldn't have done such a potentially dangerous thing. She had to at least try to justify his actions to Henry Sutherland, even if it got her nowhere.

Remembering what Pierce had mockingly said about his uncle appreciating a beautiful woman she had taken advantage of the information to put on a black sun-dress that clung alluringly to her slender curves and emphasised her heavy breasts, the high heels of her sandals showing the slender grace of her legs to advantage, her hair newly washed and loose about her shoulders, her make-up light and attractive.

'Mr Sutherland will see you now,' the

housekeeper smiled at her as she showed her in to Henry Sutherland's office.

It was a big room, had been the small drawing-room when Mrs Prendergast lived here, the walls now lined with leather-bound books, heavy leather furniture dominating one end of the room in front of the unlit fireplace, a wide desk in front of the window.

But it wasn't a fifty or sixty-year-old man who sat behind the wide mahogany leather-topped desk. Pierce wore a dark navy blue suit and white shirt, giving him a remote appearance, his expression closed, the grey eyes narrowed to icy slits as he watched her.

And as Danny looked at him it all fell into place, his remoteness, his distrust of people, the almost fanatical interest he took in the estate's security, the authority he wielded without seeming to be aware of it, the fact that, although she had made the assumption, she had never actually heard of a nephew called Pierce. That was because there wasn't one, Pierce was Henry Sutherland!

CHAPTER THREE

SHE recovered from the shock well; perhaps subconsciously she had already guessed at his identity. Pierce was so very cynical, so distrustful, it had been difficult to believe that was just because he was a relative of Henry Sutherland.

'Mr Sutherland.' She put her hand out steadily. 'Shall I continue to call you Pierce? Or would you prefer Henry? Or perhaps just Mr Sutherland?' She met his narrowed gaze blandly. 'Perhaps Mr Sutherland would be more appropriate, in the circumstances,' she added drily.

God, it was embarassing when she remembered some of the things she had said about this man to his face without realising she did so, her scorn for his passionate guarding of his privacy evident from the moment she had unthinkingly called him Howard Hughes!

'Pierce will do,' he bit out icily. 'How long have you known who I am?'

She sighed. 'Just this moment, unfortunately.'

'Unfortunately?'

'Well, you don't think I would have been so disparaging about Henry Sutherland if I'd known it was you, do you?' she said disgustedly. 'Although you must have found my candidness very amusing.'

'Not particularly,' he drawled, frowning. 'I

53

expected anger from you once you learnt the truth.'

She gave a rueful smile. 'I used up this week's anger ration last night. Why did you keep up the pretence as long as you did?'

'At first it amused me to be someone else for a change, then I found I was quite enjoying it. Being Henry Sutherland can be tiresome at times.'

'I'm sure it can.' She grimaced.

'At least you didn't question how I could possibly find it tiresome having all that money!' he rasped.

'I can imagine it could get a bit claustrophobic at times.'

'Very perceptive of you!' he drawled.

'So for a while you became Pierce Sutherland.'

'I didn't *become* him, I am him,' he rasped. 'I'm Henry Sutherland the Fourth, and that many Henrys in one family can be confusing, especially when you're a child. I became known to my family by my second name.' He grimaced. 'Thank God!'

She had to admit he didn't look much like a Henry, but with hindsight he certainly acted like the billionaire he was. His cynicism came from being treated like a god since he had inherited the Sutherland fortune at a very young age, his scepticism and distrust of people came from all those who had tried to use him over the years, his contempt for women because of all the ones that had made themselves available to him, at a price, over the last twenty years.

'I presumed Henry Sutherland would be much older somehow,' she frowned.

'Yes,' he drawled. 'Although my thirty-nine

years often weigh as heavily as seventy!'

She chewed on her bottom lip. 'So where do we go from here?'

The grey eyes narrowed warily. 'What do you mean?'

'Well, I'd hoped to appeal to Henry Sutherland on Dave Benson's behalf; knowing that Henry is you has made it a little pointless.'

Pierce's mouth twisted. 'I must say you came dressed for the part,' he derided, the heat of his gaze passing over her with insolent appraisal. 'Were you hoping to impress the old man?'

'Yes.'

He began to smile. 'Danielle Martin, what am I going to do with you?'

'Listen?' she said hopefully, encouraged by the softening of his manner.

He stood up, moving round the desk to sit on its edge. 'I'm listening.'

'Unbiasedly?'

He shook his head. 'I can't promise that.'

'Dave Benson is a good man. He——'

'What does he mean to you?'

She gave him a puzzled look. 'I don't know what you mean.'

'You can't be that naïve, Danielle,' Pierce drawled.

Colour suddenly flooded her cheeks. 'He's old enough to be my father!'

'He's only five years older than me,' he pointed out drily. 'And my feelings towards you are far from fatherly!'

'He's married . . .'

'So?'

'I may use up next week's quota of anger in a minute!' She frowned fiercely. 'I like Dave, he's a very nice man. I like his wife and children, too. I had them all over to tea one Sunday. I'm not so stupid that I don't realise a wedding ring means that neither of the couple suddenly stops looking at the opposite sex, but *I* do not get involved with married men. That's taking your damned cynicism too far!'

'Perhaps,' he acknowledged in a bored voice.

'There's no perhaps about it,' she told him impatiently. 'Dave Benson is my friend, and I stick by my friends. I'm sure that makes me an idiot in your eyes, but it's the way I am!'

'Yes,' he acknowledged uninterestedly.

'I've never met anyone as cynical as you are,' she said frustratedly.

'And I've never anyone as naïve as you are,' he scorned. 'Do you think, if the places were reversed, Benson would come to me in the same way?'

'I don't give a damn what he would do,' she snapped. 'The roles aren't reversed, and it's partially my fault he's been sacked.'

'Completely, I would have thought,' Pierce observed thoughtfully. 'You batted those long lashes at him and he didn't hesitate to break all the rules. What good would someone like that be in a real security break?' he scorned. 'One smile from a pretty woman and he would probably show her the way into the house!'

'It was because he *knew* me that he did that,' Danny insisted forcefully.

'He can't be trusted.'

'That's ridiculous.'

'No more ridiculous than what he did,' Pierce answered grimly.

She sighed her frustration. 'Do possessions mean so much to you?' she demanded disgustedly.

'What?' He glared his impatience.

'I didn't see anything at the house that was worth all this fuss!'

'No?' he asked dangerously soft.

'No.' She frowned. 'The paintings may all be originals——'

'They are.'

'And perhaps you have money in the house——'

'Some.'

She shot him an irritated glance for his interruptions. 'Private papers you wouldn't want anyone else to see——'

'Those too.' He nodded abruptly.

'But all those things are replaceable!'

'At a price,' he confirmed softly. 'But you forgot one other thing of value in the house.'

'What?' she asked scornfully.

'Me.'

'You?' Her eyes widened. 'What on earth would anyone want with you?' She was genuinely puzzled.

His mouth twisted. 'At any other time I would question the flattery of that remark,' he drawled. 'But at this moment I think impressing on you how genuine the threat of kidnapping really is may be more important.'

'Oh come on,' she dismissed, 'that sort of thing only happens in films and books.'

'You don't know what you're talking about,' Pierce accused harshly.

Her eyes flashed. 'I know that you've lived in your artificial world too long! You have people guarding you day and night, private helicopter, private jet, private hotel suites all over the world, an exclusive list of acquaintances but no real friends that I can tell, women you would rather pay to sleep with you because then you don't have to question the validity of them actually being attracted to *you* and not your money. You live your life like a character out of a book!'

'I live my life the way I've been forced to do so by society,' he corrected grimly. '*You've* lived in your safe cocoon too long if you don't know of the increase in kidnapping of prominently rich figures in recent years. I doubt the Gettys will ever forget it!'

She remembered the sensation there had been when Paul Getty's grandson had been kidnapped. But it wasn't something that happened as frequently as Pierce was implying it was, and she told him so.

'Because we've all tried to increase our security,' he pointed out grimly.

'You're being ridiculous again,' she insisted disgustedly.

His eyes were icy, his expression harsh. 'And you're being childishly naïve.'

She was breathing heavily in her frustrated anger. 'And Dave Benson?'

'His dismissal stands.' Pierce picked up a file from his desk and began flicking through it uninterestedly, obviously considering the conversation over.

It was a long way from over as far as she was concerned! 'He has a family to support,' she protested.

Broad shoulders shrugged. 'He should have thought of that sooner.' Pierce frowned down at the chart in his hand.

'Will you put that down and listen to me!' Danny snatched the file out of his hand, closing it to slam it down on the desk-top beside him. 'Now you might like to feel safe and secure in your ivory-tower,' she flared furiously. 'But us lesser mortals have to get through as best we can. Dave Benson is forty-four years old, and although that is far from being old, it's a very precarious age to be out of work in this economic climate.'

'Like I said, he should have thought of that sooner,' Pierce bit out unrelentingly.

Danny fell back a step. 'You would really do this to him?'

'He's done it to himself.'

'Because of me! All right, Mr Sutherland, obviously nothing but complete retribution will satisfy you,' she snapped erratically. 'I resign!'

'Don't be childish.'

'I'm as guilty as Dave is,' she insisted shakily. 'If he goes, so do I!'

Pierce looked at her calmly, his eyes silver-grey. 'How long did you say your family has worked at the estate?' he questioned softly.

She blushed. 'I'm third generation, work it out for yourself!' she told him resentfully.

'At least sixty years.'

'Nearer sixty-five,' she muttered.

He nodded. 'Don't you think you should go away and think your decision over rationally before breaking such a tradition?'

He sat there and callously dismissed the future of five lovely people, Dave, his wife, and their three children, and yet he told *her* to go away and think rationally. The man didn't know the meaning of the word! 'I've thought,' she snapped. 'I'm giving you a month's notice.'

He gave an impatient sigh. 'Think of your parents' disappointment if you left here.'

'They would agree that I'm doing the only thing possible in the circumstances!'

He tapped his finger-tips impatiently against the desk-top, deeply irritated by her obstinacy.

'Don't look so perplexed, Mr Sutherland,' she derided. 'I'm only the gardener.'

'A damned stupid one,' he rasped. 'Your resignation will serve no purpose. It certainly won't get Benson his job back.'

'I realise that,' she nodded. 'But I couldn't continue working here knowing I've caused someone else to lose their job.'

Pierce stood up to walk around his desk and sit down, staring thoughtfully at the pyramid of his fingers for some seconds. At last he looked up at her, cool assessment in his grey eyes. 'How much does this mean to you?'

'I can get another job,' she told him with more bravado than she felt. She probably could get herself another job, although there weren't many estates could afford the expense of full-time gardeners any more. And the thought of leaving the cottage that had been her home for the last twenty-one years totally dismayed her. But she didn't show any of that in her defiant demeanour.

'I wasn't talking of your job, I meant Benson's,' he said huskily.

Danny gave him a sharp look, frowning heavily. 'It means a great deal to me,' she answered slowly, wary of this change in him.

'How much?'

'A lot!'

He nodded. 'I've decided I'd like to go away for the weekend after all. To Paris. I want you to come with me.' He watched her with narrowed eyes.

Danny swallowed hard, moistening her lips nervously. 'Why me?'

His mouth twisted. 'I'm glad you weren't coy enough to ask why!'

'That must be more than obvious!' she snapped, her eyes a dark brown.

'Yes,' he drawled. 'And you because I want you,' he stated without emotion.

'And I don't suppose Henry Sutherland the Fourth has ever been taught he can't have everything he wants!' she scorned.

'All you have to decide is if Benson's job is worth it to you.'

'Nothing is worth that,' she assured him unhesitatingly.

'I didn't think so.' Pierce shrugged, picking up the calendar from his desk. 'A month from today will make it the tenth of August.' He glanced at her, dark brows arched. 'Is that enough time for you to find another job?'

She sucked air into her lungs, amazed at his calmness. She was in no doubt that if she had agreed to go to Paris with him both she and Dave Benson would still have their jobs now! 'It's enough time,' she said stiltedly.

He straightened. 'You wouldn't care to re-consider your decision?'

'No,' she told him tautly.

'Very well.' He nodded dismissively.

Danny walked slowly back to her cottage, feeling as if she had just tangled with a tornado. That last request for her to go to Paris with him showed her just how different their lives were, Pierce buying whatever he wanted in life, including people. It hadn't been difficult to refuse him.

Although she looked for Dave Benson during the next two days, wanting to apologise to him for the fact that she hadn't been able to help him despite her pleas on his behalf, she finally found out he had gone to France with Pierce Sutherland. She shouldn't really have been surprised, he had his notice to work out too.

Despite what she had told Pierce she still hadn't broken the news of her resignation to her family, knowing how upset her father would be. Better to be able to soften the blow with the news of another job, which she also hadn't found yet.

In the end Dave found her, coming in search of her shortly after the helicopter had brought the security men and Pierce Sutherland back to the estate. They had been gone three days, not two, as Pierce had suggested.

'I just wanted to thank you,' Dave told her

gratefully, a tall leanly attractive man with a mop of blond-grey hair, his torso firmly muscled beneath the fitted brown suit.

Thank her? 'For what?' She frowned.

'Mr Sutherland told me it was because of you that I'm keeping my job after all . . .'

'*Keeping* it?' she repeated excitedly. 'Did you say you're staying on?' she gasped disbelievingly; Pierce had been so emphatic!

He nodded, frowning at her stunned reaction. 'Mr Sutherland said it was his talk with you that influenced his change of decision.'

'Well, that's really wonderful, Dave.' She hugged him enthusiastically.

'I thought so,' he agreed slowly. 'Danny . . .?'

'Is Pierce up at the house now?'

'Yes. But——'

'I'll go and see him.' She gave Dave another hug. 'I really am pleased for you.'

Pierce had changed his mind, that was all she could think of as she almost ran over to the main house. She found him in the pool, and stood at the side until he surfaced next to her. He looked very tired, lines of weariness next to his eyes.

'You work too hard.' She said the first thing that came into her head. And then wished she hadn't. She had come here to thank him, not insult him.

His mouth twisted as he levered up out of the water, picking up a towel to walk to one of the loungers, stretching out on it. 'I don't think so, Danielle,' he derided.

'But you look tired.'

'I'm sure I do, but it's from lack of sleep, not

too much work,' he said drily. 'The companion I chose to replace you proved to be a little too enthusiastic once we reached the bedroom.'

He was trying to embarass her again, and damn him, he succeeded! No wonder he had stayed an extra day and night in Paris if his companion had been that entertaining. 'I just came to thank you for reinstating Dave Benson,' she told him woodenly. 'And now that I have I'll leave you to rest; you obviously need it!' She couldn't resist the gibe, although she wished she hadn't said it as Pierce looked amused.

'Danielle?'

She turned at the softly spoken query. 'Yes?' she said dully.

'Don't you want to know if you have your job back, too?' he drawled.

'I know I haven't,' she dismissed. 'After all, I didn't go to Paris with you.'

'You have your job back.' He scowled.

'Why?'

'Do I have to give a reason?' he rasped haughtily.

'I think so, yes.' She nodded.

'I decided to give Benson another chance because once I thought about it I realised he's probably the best security man I could possibly have now. He's had the scare of almost losing his job to shake him up, he'll be much more vigilant in future.'

She should have known his reason was as cold-blooded as that and not a genuine regret at the man losing his livelihood! Pierce had no such feelings. 'And my own job?' she prompted softly.

'I could hardly sack you and not him,' Pierce reasoned in a bored voice.

'I thought you could do anything you wanted!' Danny snapped.

His face darkened ominously. 'It seems I can't shut you up!' he rasped harshly.

'Sorry,' she muttered. She had her job back, why *didn't* she just shut up!

'I doubt that.' He scowled, standing up. 'Have dinner with me tonight.'

She frowned at the abruptness of the request. 'I thought you didn't venture out into public?'

'I meant here,' he bit out.

She shook her head. 'I can't.'

'If you mean you don't want to,' he drawled, 'then just say so.'

'Don't worry, I wouldn't hesitate,' she told him candidly. 'But I meant exactly what I said, I can't have dinner with you tonight. Gary is coming over.'

'I thought you said he didn't mean anything to you,' Pierce accused caustically.

'Not in any romantic way,' she acknowledged. 'But I am fond of him, and as I haven't been able to contact Cheryl since the weekend I'm curious to know how the two of them got on together then.'

'Curious?' he drawled.

'All right,' she admitted impatiently. 'I'm still worried about them.'

'I don't know why you don't just leave them alone to get on with it,' Pierce dismissed.

'No, you wouldn't,' she said sadly.

He looked at her with cold eyes. 'If you won't

have dinner with me tonight then how about tomorrow evening?'

'Why?'

He gave a hard derisive laugh. 'Don't be ridiculous, Danielle,' he drawled in a bored voice.

She raised surprised brows. 'Didn't your companion of the last three days provide enough amusement?'

'More than enough,' he rasped.

'Then——'

'For God's sake, Danielle,' he snapped impatiently. 'Say yes or no, but don't let's have a post mortem about it!' Anger snapped in the icy grey eyes.

'Yes,' she answered instantly. 'What time shall I come over?'

'I'll send Benson for you.'

'I'll make my own way, thank you,' she told him firmly. 'Is eight o'clock all right?'

'Yes,' he said wearily. 'Are you always this stubbornly independent?'

'Always,' she assured him happily. 'I'll see you tomorrow evening.' She smiled.

'Danielle?'

She turned as Pierce softly spoke her name, for a moment filled with a sense of how lonely he looked. But it was a loneliness of his own choosing, she told herself impatiently.

'Do you play chess?' he asked softly.

'Chess?' she repeated dumbfoundedly, this the last thing she had expected him to ask.

'It's a board-game,' he explained derisively. 'With pawns, and bishops——'

'I know what it is,' Danny cut in frustratedly.

'It just seems a strange question, that's all. Yes, I play chess.' She frowned. 'In fact you're talking to the Martin family champion.'

'I had a feeling you might say that.' Pierce grimaced. 'I'd like to give you a game tomorrow night anyway.'

'After dinner . . .?'

'Yes.'

Enigmatic was too mild a word to describe this man; he seemed to be on another plane to her! But she had never been faint-hearted, and now wasn't the time to start.

Gary was his usual uncomplicated self that evening, talking fondly of Cheryl, evidence that her sister hadn't yet spoken to him about Nigel. Cheryl was still mysteriously unavailable, and Danny couldn't help but feel vaguely disturbed by the fact. Her sister couldn't be out all the time—could she?

But Gary didn't seem at all worried about Cheryl's behaviour, so she decided she shouldn't be either. As Pierce kept telling her, it was really none of her business anyway.

Pierce. She found herself thinking about him a lot the next day, alternately anticipating and feeling apprehensive about the evening ahead. She didn't really know that much about him, except his cynicism towards the softer emotions in life. But he couldn't always have been that way, had been married once, even if it was a long time ago. She would have liked to have known the man he was then.

Choosing what to wear for her dinner with him wasn't that difficult, she only had two evening dresses, usually wearing more informal clothes even for the casual dates she received on occasion. But she had a feeling Pierce was the sort of man that 'dressed for dinner', and so she had to do the same. And as one of the dresses was a brown velvet, and the temperature was still up in the seventies, she really had only one choice. But it was a pretty dress, cream cheesecloth matched with a heavy lace, the gypsy-style neckline pulled down her arms to completely bare her shoulders and expose the creamy curve of her full breasts, fitted at her narrow waist to flow in a full skirt to just below her knees. Her legs were deeply tanned and so she left them bare, high-heeled brown sandals accompanied by a matching clutch-bag. Her hair she brushed loose and glowing, the sparkle of her eyes needing no added adornment, only a light lipgloss smoothed on her mouth.

At precisely five-to-eight she left her cottage to go over to the main house, her mouth compressing slightly as she saw Dave Benson and the two dogs waiting for her just inside the gate.

'Mr Sutherland's instructions,' Dave told her as he saw her frown.

She petted the dogs to cover her annoyance, after all it wasn't Dave's fault Pierce had gone against her request, chattering lightly to Dave as they walked over to the house.

She was shown straight into the lounge, Pierce standing by one of the windows, a drink in his hand as he turned to look at her. As she had guessed, he was wearing a dinner suit, the black material tailored to his wide shoulders and tapered waist, his silk shirt gleaming whitely. He looked very handsome, if a little more remote than usual.

Danny requested a sherry at his terse query, sinking gracefully into an armchair. So far the evening wasn't quite going as she had imagined!

'You look very lovely,' Pierce told her abruptly as he handed her the glass of sherry.

'So do you,' she returned with a mischievous gleam in her eyes.

Some of the tension seemed to go out of his shoulders as he relaxed slightly. 'How did your meeting with Gary go last night?' He sat down opposite her.

'Fine.' She nodded. 'About sending Dave Benson over for me . . .'

'I thought I was getting off too lightly,' Pierce sighed.

'Then why did you do it?'

'Habit,' he replied instantly.

It was such a simple, blunt answer that Danny didn't want to pursue it. How could she question a man on the instincts of a lifetime? 'Are we having something nice for dinner?' she asked eagerly. 'I'm afraid living on my own has made me lazy, it's all I can do to open a tin most nights.'

For a moment he looked taken aback by the sudden change of subject, and then his mouth thinned. 'You don't seem to have suffered from it,' he drawled hardily.

Danny wasn't sure she liked his tone *or* the way he was looking at her, but she didn't particularly want the evening to end before it had begun either.

'I believe we're having some sort of beef dish,' he added tersely at her continuing silence.

'Some sort of beef dish' turned out to be the tenderest most delicious tasting thinly cut strips of beef Danny had ever tasted. And as it had been preceded by prawns in avocado, and was followed by a creamy chocolate confection, she relished every mouthful of the meal, barely having room for the strong coffee that was served to her while Pierce enjoyed a brandy. In contrast to her own enjoyment of the meal Pierce ate sparingly, almost uninterestedly, and she couldn't stop herself criticising him because of it.

'Didn't you *like* the meal?' She made it sound as if he had to be insane if he hadn't.

'It was adequate,' he said in a bored voice.

She gave a disgusted snort. 'You ought to try living with me for a week, then you would know what adequate is all about!'

He raised dark brows over mocking eyes. 'Are you propositioning me?'

She gave an embarrassed glance at the butler, a middle-aged man almost as haughty as his employer. 'That will be all, Masters,' Pierce dismissed the man without even looking up, still watching Danny.

She chuckled once they were alone in the intimacy of the small dining-room. 'You've left the poor man burning with curiosity as to what my answer is going to be!'

'*I'm* burning with curiosity as to what your answer will be!'

She looked at him reproachfully. 'You know very well it was a perfectly innocent remark.'

'Pity,' he drawled.

'You wouldn't say that if you really did have to eat my cooking for a week!'

'It wasn't the cooking I was interested in,' he told her softly.

'Are you always as sexually orientated as this?' she said irritably.

'As a rule I can't say I give it that much thought,' he admitted with a frown.

'That's because too many women make themselves available to you!'

'You haven't.'

'Because I'm not,' she answered simply.

'Would you like that game of chess now?'

She blinked. 'Now?'

'Yes.'

'I—Well, I—Yes.' She frowned her puzzlement. 'If that's what you want to do.' She nodded.

The chess pieces were beautifully carved out of jade and onyx, the board of a similar design. Danny touched the jade pieces lovingly as she put them on the board.

'Are you as good as you like to think you are?'

She looked across the low table at Pierce. 'I didn't say I was good, only that I am the family champion.'

He nodded. 'How about a small wager on the outcome?'

'You want to bet on the result of this chess game?' she asked warily.

'It makes it more—interesting.'

'That depends on what the wager is,' Danny said drily, not at all enamoured of the gleam of intent in his eyes.

'You.'

She gave a splutter of laughter. 'I had a feeling last night that this was what you had in mind when you asked if I played.'

'You find it funny?' He scowled.

'I'm interested to hear what I get if I win.' Amusement sparkled in her eyes.

'What is it you want?' he asked in a disgruntled voice.

She pretended to give it some thought. 'A Ferrari, I think,' she mocked. 'A red one.'

'It's yours,' Pierce told her instantly.

'Pierce, I was only joking,' she lightly teased him.

'I wasn't,' he said grimly. 'No woman has ever asked for a Ferrari before, but it's less boring than jewellery.'

'You do this sort of thing, often, get a woman in bed with you by playing chess with them?'

His mouth twisted. 'Most of the women I've met over the years wouldn't know a chess-board from backgammon!'

'I'm not going to bed with a man on the result of a chess game either!' she gasped.

'You could win the Ferrari.'

'I told you, I don't really want a Ferrari!'

'Then what do you want?' His voice was raised angrily, his eyes silver. 'Just tell me what you want so that I can make love to you!'

CHAPTER FOUR

'You could try asking.'

He looked up at her sharply, searchingly, Danny looking steadily back at him. 'Well?' he finally said gruffly.

'I have to say no——'

'What are you, some sort of damned tease?' His arm swung out and he knocked all the chess pieces off the board, cursing angrily as he saw what he had done. 'You tell me to ask and then turn me down!'

She sighed. 'I didn't turn you down.' She shook her head. 'You just didn't let me finish. I have to say no for now,' she continued softly, 'because I truly don't believe we've known each other long enough to start such an intimate relationship. But I am attracted to you, and I——' She drew in a deep breath. 'I believe I might one day like to go to bed with you.'

'One day?' he prompted hardly.

'When we know each other better.' She nodded.

'How well do you have to know a man before you go to bed with him?'

She wished she knew; she had never even contemplated it before. But she wasn't going to lie about being attracted to this man, he would only have to kiss her again to be aware of it.

'Better than I know you now, obviously.' She grimaced.

'Move in with me,' he said forcefully.

Her eyes widened. 'I only live half a mile away,' she derided. 'Besides, I have my work to do.'

'Let Zacky Boone take over for a few weeks.'

A few weeks. Was he putting a time limit on their relationship before it had begun? 'I don't think so, Pierce.' She shook her head.

'I want you.'

'Yes, I know,' she sighed. 'I'm attracted to you, too——'

'I'm not just attracted to you,' he bit out savagely. 'I burn with wanting you. All the time I was with Marie-Clare in Paris I was wishing she were you,' he admitted harshly, as if he didn't particularly like the fact. 'I want you in my bed, Danielle! I want to touch you and I want you to touch me, too.'

Danny swallowed hard at the image that conjured up in her mind, her nipples tautened beneath the cheesecloth material. 'Talking in that way can only make things worse——'

'Because neither of us wants to talk!' His eyes glittered with desire. 'I can guarantee that this time you wouldn't feel *empty*—far from it!'

It was obvious from this statement that the comment she had once made about him had hurt more than he had shown at the time, and the insult had been far from forgotten. 'Emotionally I would,' she answered softly. 'And that's what's important.'

Pierce's mouth twisted. 'If you think that in time I'll fall in love with you you're in for a great disappointment.'

She shook her head sadly. 'I'm hoping I'll fall in love with you; because that's the only reason

I'll ever make love with you. It wouldn't be making love otherwise, would it?' she reasoned logically.

'Love rarely enters into it,' he said disgustedly.

'It has to for me, I'm afraid.' She grimaced.

'Even if I'll never love you in return?'

She shrugged. 'It's the risk everyone takes.'

'I prefer not to do so.'

'You're lucky if you have the choice,' she chided softly. 'Most people aren't that lucky.'

'It isn't a matter of luck,' he bit out coldly. 'Love is a vulnerable emotion I never intend to feel again!'

Danny presumed he had once loved his wife. And by the sound of it it hadn't been a happy marriage. He had never remarried, so presumably the one time had been enough to show him it wasn't for him.

'You shouldn't have given me my job back so easily,' she teased him. 'Now that just might have worked as blackmail now that I've had time to see how sparse the jobs like mine are.'

Instead of the lessening of tension she had been hoping for Pierce's scowl deepened. 'I didn't use blackmail on you concerning Benson's reinstatement,' he rasped. 'I offered you an exchange.'

'My body for his job,' she scorned.

'It seemed very fair to me.'

She could see that it did, that he considered it had been a very good deal! Poor Pierce, his whole outlook was warped by the users he had met in his life. 'I suppose it was,' she accepted without rancour, going down on her knees to begin picking up the chess pieces.

'Leave them,' Pierce ordered impatiently.

'Don't be silly——'

'I said leave them!' He pulled her roughly to her feet, his expression gentling as he looked down at her startled face. 'Why did you have to be so young?' he groaned.

'I don't really think age has anything to do with it,' she murmured softly.

'No,' he admitted raggedly. 'It's your idealism that's the stumbling block!

'I have your respect,' she claimed. 'Don't I?'

He looked angry. 'Is that all you want from me, respect?'

She smiled. 'It's a start.'

'To what?' He put her away from him, eyeing her warily.

Danny shrugged. 'To liking.'

'You mean loving,' he scorned derisively. 'That route isn't for me, Danielle.'

She believed him, knew that he had gone all the years since his marriage without loving another woman; she certainly wasn't going to be the woman to achieve the impossible after all this time. 'How long is it since you had a relationship, Pierce?'

His brows rose. 'I got back from Paris only yesterday . . .'

'I said a relationship, Pierce, not a convenience,' she corrected gently.

Irritation darkened his face. 'You mean talking together, laughing together, sitting together enjoying the silence, loving together?' he derided. 'More years than I care to think about!'

'Of course, you don't trust anyone,' she remembered sadly.

'No, I don't,' he confirmed hardly. 'Now, are you going to bed with me or aren't you?'

'I aren't—I mean, I'm not,' Danny said awkwardly, thrown a little off-balance by his uncharacteristic aggression. 'Do you still want to have a game of chess?'

'Hell, no!' He scowled. 'I believe the evening is at an end.'

Her eyes widened. 'You're throwing me out?'

'Yes.'

'That isn't very polite of you.'

'I'm not feeling very polite,' he growled, his hands thrust into his trousers pockets. 'In fact, I'm feeling very impolite!'

She couldn't hold back her humour, starting to chuckle, then to laugh outright.

'You look like a little boy denied a treat,' she teased his disgruntled mood.

'I feel like a big boy denied a treat!'

She laughed again, feeling a thrill of pleasure when Pierce began to chuckle, too. He really was very handsome when he relaxed a little. 'Let's play chess,' she suggested impulsively. 'I feel like beating you,' she added challengingly.

'Isn't once in an evening enough?' he mocked drily, starting to arrange the pieces on the board.

Her mouth quirked. 'I've only delayed the inevitable, we both know that.'

He frowned. 'Don't let me hurt you, Danielle,' he said gruffly.

'I told you, I won't have the choice.'

He looked at her quietly for several tension filled seconds, suddenly drawing in a ragged breath. 'Jade or onyx?' he finally asked abruptly.

She opted for jade, keeping up light-hearted chatter as they prepared the board, not allowing herself the luxury of thought until they faced each other across the table. Even then she wouldn't allow herself to dwell on the fact that she was already falling in love with this man.

'Have you heard from your nephew lately?' She put the question casually.

Pierce made his opening move, looking up at her curiously. 'Nigel?'

Her mouth twisted. 'I believe Henry Sutherland only has one nephew,' she mocked.

'You didn't seem angry by my deception at the time,' he frowned.

'I'm not angry now,' she shook her head, 'I'm sure it was fun being someone else for a while.'

'Yes,' he agreed abruptly. 'And why should you want to know about Nigel?'

She shrugged. 'I haven't been able to speak to Cheryl for several days, and I—well, I just wondered if you knew anything about them?'

'Nigel is at my office in New York,' Pierce supplied absently, studying the board.

'Then why isn't Cheryl answering the telephone?' she muttered to herself.

Pierce looked up sharply. 'Are you genuinely worried about her?'

'No, I— Yes,' she sighed. 'She's never at home any more.'

'Maybe she's found someone else to amuse her while Nigel's away,' he dismissed.

'I know you don't mean to be insulting, Pierce,' she said forcefully. 'But you are!'

'Sorry,' he said drily. 'Would you like me to make enquiries in London?'

'No,' she sighed again. 'Cheryl wouldn't like that.'

'It would be done discreetly.'

Having someone go and spy on her young sister? No, she couldn't do that, no matter how concerned she was. 'I don't think so, thank you.' She shook her head, looking down at the chess-board, where she already seemed to be losing rather badly. 'I'm glad we didn't make the wager!' she said with self-derision. 'You're too good at this!'

'That's what Sa——' He broke off, his expression harshly angry.

'Yes?' Danny prompted softly.

'Nothing,' he bit out forcefully.

Danny moistened her lips. 'You used to play chess with your wife?'

'I never talk about my wife!'

He had been going to talk about her just now—and he was furiously angry with himself because of it. 'What was her name?' she asked gently.

'Sally.' Pierce stood up, his movements jerky.

'You loved her very much,' she realised with concern.

'Of course I——' He glared at her with narrowed eyes. 'Why are you asking these questions?'

'Because she's part of you, and I want to know all of you.'

'She was dead before you even went to school,' he dismissed harshly.

It sounded a very long time when he put it like that! 'You've been alone all that time?'

Pierce frowned. 'You aren't going to subject me to the usual inadequate platitudes?' he rasped.

'You've just said it, they are inadequate. Only you can know the extent of your loss—or not.'

'Yes,' he acknowledged flatly.

Danny could see how disturbed he was by the conversation, she stood up. 'Why don't we finish this game another night? Or you can take it that you won, if you like,' she teased. 'You're not in my class!'

He gave an impatient snort. 'This has been a hell of an evening for you.'

'I've enjoyed it.'

'You couldn't have done.' He shook his head derisively. 'I've handled this thing with the finesse of a callow youth; I should have seduced you into bed, not bluntly asked or tried to buy you!'

She smiled at his disgust with himself. 'Maybe next time,' she mocked.

'You're on your guard now.' He grimaced.

Danny laughed softly. 'Come over for dinner tomorrow,' she invited. 'I'll open a couple of tins and throw us a meal together.'

'That sounds——'

'Awful,' she finished. 'I know.' She nodded happily. 'Actually, I'm not too bad a cook. Gary had no complaints the other night, anyway. He wasn't to know I opened a tin of soup, bought one of those pre-cooked roast meats, and made a packet meringue. As far as he was concerned I'd cooked him a meal fit for a king.'

Pierce was chuckling softly by the time she had finished. 'Tinned soup and pre-cooked food sounds delicious.'

She made a face at him. 'You're sure you wouldn't rather invite me over here again?' she coaxed. 'You must have the best cook in the country!'

'You may have noticed, I'm a little tired of Cordon Bleu cooking,' he said drily.

'In that case you're perfectly welcome to sample the delights of my kitchen.'

'I'll walk you home.' He smiled.

It was a beautiful summer's evening, the moon very bright in the starlit sky, the man at her side perfect, too. He didn't seem like Henry Sutherland the Fourth at this moment, just a very attractive man who had a surprisingly dry sense of humour that seemed to have come as a surprise to him, too!

'How long since you walked a girl home after a date?' she teased as they entered her garden, the scent of roses sweet and heady.

He seemed to give the question some thought as they reached her door. 'Hmmph years.' He ran a hand over his mouth as he said the actual number.

Danny laughed delightedly. 'That's cheating,' she chided indulgently.

'The answer, I discover, is a little too ageing.' His tone was one of disgust.

'You aren't old.' She touched the hardness of his cheek, pleased when he didn't flinch from her as he had that first night by the pool. 'You're mature.'

'And do you like mature men?'

'I like *you*,' she told him candidly, reaching up to kiss him lightly on the lips. 'Thank you for a nice evening, I hope tomorrow will be as enjoyable for you.'

'Is this the part of the evening where I get to kiss you good night?' he drawled derisively.

Her eyes glowed mischievously. 'This is the part,' she encouraged softly.

His lips possessed hers gently, moving searchingly against her, one hand cupping her cheek as he made no effort to pull her in to his arms.

Danny drew in a shaky breath as he drew back. 'Would it disturb you if I were to use the lawn-mower tonight?' she asked huskily.

'You need to think?'

'Yes.'

'About us?'

'Yes.'

'Then go ahead,' he invited with satisfaction. 'I'm happy that you need to think about it.'

'You have me half in love with you already,' Danny admitted seriously.

'You know that isn't what I want.' Pierce scowled.

'Why should it bother you if it gets me in your bed?' She smoothed the frown from his brow. 'Don't let it worry you, Pierce, I probably just have a case of indigestion!'

He shook his head, smiling. 'You certainly know how to flatter a man! Indigestion, indeed,' he muttered indignantly.

She knew very well it wasn't indigestion, but she could see that he didn't welcome her honesty about this, that he really did prefer not to have emotions involved in a relationship with him. And so far he seemed to have met women who

were agreeable to the brief relationship he
wanted. So far? She knew she wasn't half in love
with him at all, that somewhere during the
evening she had fallen wholly in love with this
complex, strangely vulnerable, man.

Dinner was a success, mainly because she had
raided her freezer of several of the goodies she
had bought the last time she had gone in to town.
The prawn cocktail was already prepared, Danny
only had to put together a salad to go with the
quiche and baked potatoes, and warm through an
apple pie to go with the ice cream.

Pierce wasn't formally dressed this evening, he
arrived in faded denims and a loose cotton shirt
the same blue-grey colour of his eyes. She was
glad about that, because she had organised their
meal on her garden-set on the patio outside the
lounge, sure they would have looked ridiculous
sitting in the gaily covered plastic chairs in formal
evening wear!

'It looks a lot more comfortable and relaxed in
films.' Danny swished away another fly.

Pierce laughed softly. 'I've enjoyed myself.
You really will have to tell me the name of your
chef,' he added mockingly, having eaten all the
food put in front of him.

'I'll pass on your compliments,' she told him in
an exaggeratedly haughty voice.

'Do that,' he taunted.

'I wonder if the shop could have "By
appointment to Henry Sutherland" printed on
the boxes,' she mused. 'Think what it could do
for sales.'

'I think that only happens with royalty.' He pulled a face.

'Well, you're pretty famous yourself. Come to think of it,' she frowned, 'I really don't know how I had the nerve to serve that food up to you.' She grimaced.

'I told you, I enjoyed it.'

He did look very relaxed, the coldness gone from his eyes, an indulgent smile playing about his firm lips. 'Now what can I offer you in the way of after-dinner entertainment?' She stood up to clear away, closing the kitchen door on the small amount of washing-up they had made.

'Isn't that rather a leading question in the circumstances?' he drawled.

'That depends.' She met his gaze across the room.

Pierce was suddenly very still. 'On what?'

'On where you want it to lead to.'

'Come here, Danielle,' he invited gruffly.

She didn't hesitate, going straight into his arms, denim against denim, cotton against cotton. 'Pierce, I . . .'

'We don't need to talk,' he silenced her.

She was aware of the throbbing of his thighs before his mouth gently claimed hers, his desire let loose as she surrendered to him, her passion more than a match for his.

'No bra,' he murmured as he pushed her blouse off her shoulders to reveal her bared breasts. 'I like that,'

She cradled his head to her as he suckled on her nipple. 'I did it for you,' she gasped.

He looked up at her. 'You planned this?'

'I want it.'

'Danielle . . .'

'Please, Pierce, let's enjoy each other,' she urged.

'But . . .'

'Are you usually this difficult to seduce?' she lightly teased.

'I need to know.'

'You said you only needed me to want you,' she cut in firmly. 'And I do.' She didn't want to answer questions about her feelings for him, knew Pierce was stubborn enough to refuse them both once she had confessed to loving him.

He only hesitated for several more seconds before his mouth claimed hers once again and there was no more talk, only soft murmurs of encouragement and appreciation, leaving their clothes in a scattered heap on the lounge floor as they went upstairs to Danny's bedroom.

'Can I leave on the bedside lamp?' Pierce gazed down hungrily at the cream and honey-gold hues of her nakedness. 'I want to watch you as I make love to you.'

'I want to watch you, too,' she told him huskily, boldly admiring the hard plains of his body.

He nodded his satisfaction. 'I'm glad you aren't a shy young virgin; I'm too old to cope with *that* feminine coyness!

She certainly wasn't coy, or shy, but she was . . .

'God, Danielle, I want to feel you shudder and tremble about me,' Pierce's eyes were dark pools of desire. 'I can't wait any longer!'

'Pierce, I need to talk to you——'

'As I said, not now,' he mocked, pinning her arms within the circle of his. 'There, you have to be silent now!'

She appreciated his teasing about her talking with her hands, but she really did have to . . .

God, what was he doing to her now! Every inch of her torso knew the touch of his lips as he sat down on the bed to pull her in between his legs, the tugging motion on her breasts causing a warmth between her thighs, one of his hands cupping her there.

Their movements were slow and unhurried as each learnt the secrets of the other's body, Danny guided by instinct as she caused him to shudder for possession, her legs around his back as she guided him into her. Her teeth bit into the firm flesh of his shoulder as the sharp pain preceded his complete filling of her, she felt him tense and stop, attempt to draw back. Her legs closed more firmly about him as she clung to him.

'Danielle, you're——'

'I know what I *was*, Pierce.' Fiery brown eyes looked up at him. 'I also know I'm not going to let you cheat us both of what we want.' She began to move beneath him, feeling him harden to his former tautness. 'Your body won't let you deny us,' she realised triumphantly as he began to move above her.

Pierce's mouth was on hers as the trembling began deep inside her, as an aching pleasure unlike anything else she had ever known spread from her thighs to every particle of her body, as she shuddered about him in climactic fulfilment,

feeling the hard tension of his body before he
gave in to his own need in wave after wave of
consuming pleasure.

She ached, she was a little sore, but she had
never felt more wonderfully alive in her life!

'Oh, Pierce.' Her hands convulsed on his back
as the aftershock possessed her. 'Pierce!' She
laughed her feelings of complete freedom. 'It was
wonderful! Beautiful! I've never—Pierce?' she
suddenly sensed his wariness. 'Pierce wasn't it
good for you?' She couldn't believe he hadn't
shared in that unbelievable sensation.

'It was much more than good.' He lay beside
her, tenderly smoothing the hair at her brow.
'We've just shared something special, something
I've never known before with any other woman.'

She frowned as he still looked troubled. 'You
aren't angry because I was a virgin . . .?'

'No! Not angry, exactly,' he amended shakily.
'At least, not with you.'

'Who then?' She frowned. He certainly wasn't
making much sense!

'Myself,' he grated.

'But I wanted you——'

'I'm not angry because I took your virginity;
that's your prerogative to give to whichever man
you choose,' he rasped harshly. 'I'm angry with
myself because I take a primitive pleasure in
knowing I was your first lover. I've always told
myself physical faithfulness isn't important. But
I'm sure that if you took another lover now I'd
want to kill him!'

She touched his cheek lovingly. 'I've waited
twenty-one years for you, I don't think I'll be in

a desperate hurry to find someone else,' she teased lightly. 'I've entrusted myself to you.'

'I know that,' he bit out. 'Which makes this all the harder to tell you.'

Danny gave him a puzzled frown; what could possibly be so important after what they had just shared? 'What is it, Pierce?'

He sighed. 'After I left you last night I decided to telephone Nigel in New York, see if he knew anything about your sister. He has Cheryl with him in New York.'

CHAPTER FIVE

SHE moistened suddenly dry lips. 'Why didn't you tell me earlier? You had plenty of opportunity during dinner.'

He drew in a ragged breath. 'I told myself it was none of my business. It just became so,' he added grimly.

'Not because we made love together——'

'It was more than that and you know it,' Pierce rasped.

'How could I? she said dully.

'If I tell you that most times after I've had sex with a woman I feel completely alone. I know little real satisfaction, I often can't even remember the name of the woman I'm with—I usually don't even care! I feel self-disgust . . .'

'Stop!' she pleaded shakily.

'A few minutes ago we made love,' he told her harshly. 'And when it was over I wanted to hold you, protect you, and then make love to you again. I still feel that way. And that makes your sister my business too!' he explained forcefully.

'How long have they been in New York together?' she asked quietly.

'Four days.'

'How could Cheryl have been so *stupid*? What if Gary finds out?' she groaned.

'Nigel tells me they're in love,' Pierce said

drily. 'So I very much doubt if your sister cares if her fiancé finds out.'

'Mum and Dad will be furious if they hear about it!'

'Are you going to tell them?'

Danny glared at him. 'My sister may be stupid, but I'm not going to add to her problems!'

'Sorry.' He looked suitably repentant.

'When are they coming home?'

'The end of the week.'

She shook her head. 'They have to come back *now*; I have to try and talk some sense into Cheryl,' she added intently.

'Danielle, what if they really are in love with each other?'

'Cheryl owes it to Gary to tell him the truth,' she bit out tautly. 'She owes him that!'

'Yes,' Pierce agreed heavily. 'I'll have Nigel brought back immediately.'

She looked at him with a frown. 'Brought back?'

His mouth twisted. 'Well, I doubt if he actually wants to return just yet,' he mocked drily. 'I wouldn't, if it were you with me.'

'Then we'll just have to wait until they want to come home,' she decided. 'I couldn't put Cheryl through the humiliation of being escorted back!'

'The two of you are very close, aren't you?'

'Not close enough, obviously,' she said disgustedly.

'Don't feel too bad about it, Danielle,' Pierce soothed gently. 'I doubt you've told her about me either, have you?'

She blushed at the truth of that. 'There wasn't really anything to tell until tonight!'

'All the more shocking,' he softly mocked.

She gave him an impatient look. 'Can I help it if you're so incredibly sexy?'

He relaxed a little as some of the tension left her. 'Maybe Nigel has inherited some of my devastating charm!'

'Aren't you a little young to be his uncle? Nigel has to be in his late twenties at least.'

'Thirty,' Pierce confirmed. 'My sister Chloe is ten years older than me, and she married very young. She was only nineteen when Nigel was born. I used to think he was my brother when I came home for the school holiday.' He grimaced.

'There's just you and your sister?' She really didn't know that much about his personal life.

'Yes,' he answered abruptly. 'Chloe is married to Clive Patrick, the inventor.'

She had heard of the other man, knew that he was almost as wealthy as Pierce himself, had invented several kitchen appliances that were in worldwide use. 'He's very clever.' She frowned.

'So is Nigel. But he chooses to channel his intelligence into the world of finance. He'll make a fitting heir for me one day.'

'But you're still young . . .'

'And I'll never marry again.' He moved so that he was looking down at her. 'No matter how often we're together like this I'll never marry you, Danielle.'

She had known that, realised that if he were going to marry again that he would have done so by now; Sally had been dead sixteen years. 'I wasn't hinting, Pierce,' she chided. 'I was just pointing out that you won't need an heir for a long time yet.'

He sighed. 'I was being conceited thinking what I did.'

'No,' she smiled. 'You very correctly guessed that I love you . . .'

'Danielle . . .'

'I'm sure you've noticed I'm a very straight-speaking person,' she derided. 'I'm not going to pretend to be blasé about this relationship, it just isn't in me. I'll take what you can give, when you can give it. I'll make no ties on you, ever.'

'That's a very one-sided arrangement.' Pierce frowned darkly.

She shrugged. 'At least you don't have to pay me to like you,' she reminded him of the claim he had once made about the many women in his life. 'Don't you realise how much you belittle yourself by indulging in such businesslike relationships? You're worthy of deeper feelings than that, Pierce!'

'Am I?' he said bitterly.

'Yes,' she insisted with certainty. 'If you were as selfish as you pretend to be my initiation tonight would have been painful and completely lacking in tenderness, and we both know it wasn't that.'

He shook his head, touching her slightly swollen lips. 'Even Sally wasn't a virgin when I met her.'

'I've lived a very sheltered life.' Danny attempted to tease.

Pierce gave her a look that told her he knew very well of the invitations she must have received from men in the past, invitations she had felt no temptation to accept. 'Then I suppose I'd better give you another lesson in pleasing your man.' He pretended irritation with the idea, his eyes dark with desire.

'Oh thank you.' Danny feigned wide-eyed gratitude. 'You're so good to me.'

'You're so good *for* me,' Pierce muttered almost disbelievingly. 'No woman has ever made me so aware of the sense of the ridiculous, or made me laugh, the way you do.'

'Not at this precise moment, I hope,' she mocked.

'The only thing I find ridiculous about this moment is the amount of time we've wasted talking about the arrangement when we could be doing something about it!'

'Oh, I'm not sure my poor battered body is up to another lesson just yet.'

'God, I'm sorry! I wasn't thinking. I've never had to deal with——'

'I was joking, Pierce,' she laughed at his worried expression. 'I was beginning to think you were *too* mature. Maybe a younger man . . .'

'I think you must have been behind the word provocative,' he growled, pinning her to the bed beneath him. 'I'll just have to prove I'm not too old for you!'

He did that several times during the night, seeming insatiable, carrying her back to bed even after they had taken a bath together. It was almost noon by the time Danny, fully dressed now, pulled back the bedroom curtains to let in the sunlight. She frowned as she saw the man standing at her garden gate.

'Don Bridgeman is hovering downstairs,' she frowned, turning back to Pierce as he finished buttoning his shirt. 'Do you think he's nervous about coming in?' she teased.

Pierce joined her at the window, eyes narrowed as he looked out at the other man. 'He doesn't want to come in,' he dismissed, turning away.

She glanced back at Don. 'Then what's he doing out there?'

'What does any Head of Security usually do?' He shrugged.

She frowned. 'Guarding you . . .?'

'Yes, Danielle.'

'Has he been standing out there all night?' she gasped disbelievingly.

Pierce shook his head. 'Benson is on night duty, remember. About tonight——'

'Are you telling me Dave Benson stood outside my cottage all night?' Colour burned in her cheeks. 'That he was waiting there while we—when we—Tell me he didn't, Pierce!' She groaned her dismay.

He became suddenly still. 'I'm not prepared to lie to you,' he said quietly.

'You mean he was there!' She flinched. 'How am I supposed to face any of them again?'

'Are you ashamed?'

'No!'

'Then you're giving a very good impression of it,' he rasped grimly, his eyes narrowed.

'I'm not ashamed,' she insisted firmly. 'It's just that those men have become friends of mine the last months. They may be used to standing guard while you spend the night with your latest woman, but it's never been *me* before! Don't you want any private life, Pierce?'

'I have a private life,' he bit out. 'Benson and Bridgeman were outside, what happened between us was completely private.'

'You don't need much of an imagination to know what happened!'

Pierce's mouth was tight, his jaw clenched. 'If you can't live with the way I am maybe we had better end this now.'

Her fiery protest died on her lips as she saw the expression in his eyes, a puzzling mixture of desperation and wariness. And suddenly she realised how nervous Pierce was of a relationship between them.

'I can live with it,' she told him softly. 'About tonight . . .?' she prompted his half-finished statement.

'I have an appointment in London this afternoon, I'm not sure what time it will end. I may spend the night in town,' he added coolly.

The business appointment hadn't seemed that important a short time ago, in fact they wouldn't be out of bed now if Danny hadn't insisted she had to get to work. Pierce was backing away from what they had between them!

Danny moved in to his arms, feeling his instant reponse to her as she pressed her body close to his. 'I shall be waiting up for you.' She placed butterfly kisses along the hard line of his jaw.

'I told you——'

'I'll wait up for you, anyway,' she murmured against the lobe of his ear. 'You might manage to get home.'

'I'll try.' He put her firmly away from him, his expression bleak. 'Don't love me, Danielle.'

'You know I already do,' she stated softly.

'I'll only hurt you.'

Danny shrugged. 'It's all part of living.'

'You're too young to really mean that,' he rasped.

'My parents would tell you I was born old.' She shook her head. 'I was philosophising on life while still in the cradle!'

His silver gaze lingered on her slightly swollen lips before he went to the top of the stairs. 'In experience, and I don't mean physically,' he rasped bleakly, 'you're still in the cradle. Life doesn't fall into such neat little patterns.'

'I know that,' she grinned. 'No one could call *us* a neat relationship.'

'Danielle . . .'

'Go outside and assure Bridgeman I haven't poisoned you while you slept,' she mockingly interrupted his impatient exclamation. Pierce looked even angrier by her taunt, and she laughed softly. 'If I kill you with anything it will be with love!'

He shook his head, running lightly down the stairs, the back door closing softly seconds later as he left. Danny stood at the window and watched as Pierce and Don Bridgeman walked back to the main house, the two men chatting easily together.

Embarrassed or not she intended making a special point of seeing Dave Benson and Don Bridgeman as soon as she could, liking both men, and still wanting their respect.

Her heart gave an excited leap when she heard the return of the helicopter shortly after nine, running to the window just in time to see the huge metal bird hover before landing.

She expected Pierce to be over to see her as soon as he had showered and changed, but when ten o'clock came round and he still hadn't made an appearance she felt the anger rise within her. If Pierce thought he could treat her like a one-night stand he was in for a shock; she wouldn't be treated that shabbily.

Kilpatrick and Ferdinand accompanied her over to the manor house as she strode across the perfectly kept lawn, a furious figure in white shorts and white lace top, her hair once more secured in the single braid, her eyes sparkling with temper. Pierce wouldn't find her a meek insecure woman who stayed away because she thought he didn't want her any more. She *knew* he wanted her.

She didn't hesitate at the french doors that led into the brightly lit lounge, striding furiously inside. The next few seconds would have been funny if they weren't so disastrous. Kilpatrick and Ferdinand had followed her into the lounge, their teeth baring as they began to growl at the man and woman in the lounge with Pierce. The young woman took one look at the huge dogs, gave a shrill scream before climbing up on the sofa, the middle-aged man moving warily behind the sofa, his gaze never leaving the two dogs. Pierce looked coldly angry for several seconds before humour took over, and then he had trouble holding back a smile.

'Now that you've treated my guests to a scene straight out of a horror movie, perhaps you wouldn't mind dismissing the dogs,' he drawled softly, 'then Clarissa can get down off the furniture!'

She ordered the dogs outside, having no difficulty stifling her own humour as she turned to see Pierce helping the petite blonde down off the sofa, his arm about her protectively as she leaned in to him, looking up at him gratefully.

'Where did you come from?'

Danny hadn't been aware of the man's approach until she turned at the sound of his Texas drawl, looking up into a face still handsome despite being in its forties, the blond hair silvered to grey at the temples, the blue eyes twinkling merrily. 'Well, I'm not the "fairy from the bottom of the garden",' she mocked her stature. 'Although I do live there.'

'Are the dogs yours?'

'Pierce's,' she answered abruptly, the beautiful blonde patting delicately at her cheeks with Pierce's handkerchief now. 'They're guard-dogs,' she added absently, still watching Pierce with the other woman.

'And do they guard you for Pierce?'

She frowned at the suggestion in his tone. 'I can look after myself,' she snapped.

He smiled. 'I'll just bet you can.'

'Which is more than your girlfriend seems able to do,' she bit out as Pierce murmured soothingly to the other woman.

'Clarissa is my daughter,' he corrected softly. 'I'm Paul Banyon,' he introduced.

'Danny Martin,' she returned heavily, wishing Pierce would stop touching the beautiful Clarissa.

Paul watched his daughter, too. 'She tends to

over-react; I blame it on the Swiss finishing-school I sent her to,' he drawled. 'I quite enjoyed your little show with the dogs.'

'Is that why you hid behind the sofa?' she taunted.

He laughed softly. 'It isn't polite to remind a man of a moment of weakness.'

Her mouth twisted. 'Have I seemed very polite to you so far?'

'You've seemed delightful,' Paul chuckled. 'I can't remember the last time a woman interested me so much.'

'Then you must lead a very dull life!'

'On the contrary,' he smiled without rancour, 'I was a hell-raiser before you were born.'

Paul Banyon! She remembered him now, heir to his grandfather's oil empire in Texas he had inherited billions at the age of eighteen, had been involved in more scandals since then than Danny could possibly remember, married at twenty to a Las Vegas showgirl he had managed to have one child, a daughter, in the brief two-year marriage before his wife ran off with a rodeo star. There had been an endless succession of women since then. And the way he was looking at her she had the feeling he had chosen her to be the next one!

'I see you've realised who I am,' he mocked as she looked at him warily now.

'Mr Banyon.' She shook his hand politely. 'And I'm Pierce's gardener.'

He chuckled disbelievingly. 'Really?'

'Yes—really.'

Blond brows rose. 'I had hoped he had provided you for me.'

She looked up at him with cold eyes. 'Pierce may provide those sort of services for his guests, I wouldn't know, but you can be assured I'm not one of them!'

Contrition darkened his eyes, his humour instantly gone. 'Danny . . .'

She pulled away from him to cross the room, coming to a halt in front of Pierce, his arm still about Clarissa Banyon. 'I don't know what sort of games you're playing,' she snapped contemptuously, 'but I want no part of them!' She turned on her heel.

'Danielle!'

She turned back to Pierce with tears in her eyes. 'What were you doing, Pierce, trying me out first before recommending me to your friends?'

'Danny, I didn't mean——'

'You can tell me later exactly what you said to her to make her believe such a thing.' Pierce turned savagely on the other man. 'And you can consider our business deal off; I don't deal with people who insult special people in my life.' He put Clarissa firmly away from him. 'Danielle . . .?'

'Business deal . . .?' Danny repeated shakily.

His gaze was gentle on her face. 'I told you I had a business meeting this afternoon, Banyon was it. I invited them back to conclude the deal before they return to the States tomorrow.'

'Oh dear,' Danny grimaced at her wrong assumptions. 'I thought— Oh dear,' she groaned again.

'I was going to come over later,' Pierce told her gently.

She looked at him pleadingly. 'You see, I thought, because of earlier . . .'

'I know what you thought,' he acknowledged softly, ignoring their audience. 'And maybe with some women I might have acted that way, but not with you.'

She looked at Paul Banyon and his daughter. 'I'm so sorry,' she said awkwardly. 'You must think I'm some sort of escaped lunatic.'

'I think Sutherland is a very lucky man,' Paul smiled.

Clarissa Banyon, a complete antithesis to her father, looked shocked by Danny's aggression. 'Could I possibly go to my room now, Pierce?' Her Texas drawl wasn't as strong either, probably mellowed by her Swiss education. 'I feel a little—tired.'

'Stop being so damned delicate,' her father snapped irritably. 'Maybe you've been *too* protected.'

'Daddy!'

'Her husband-to-be doesn't know what he's getting,' Paul said disgustedly, turning to Pierce and Danny. 'We can go back to London tonight if you would prefer it.'

'No! Please!' Danny was the one to answer, looking up pleadingly at Pierce. 'This whole silly thing is my mistake. Mr Banyon was very polite. But I took one look at you with Miss Banyon . . .'

'And she almost called back the dogs,' Paul drawled with relish. 'I think I'd question their loyalty, Sutherland.'

'I don't need to,' Pierce said softly. 'They

would protect Danielle to the death. And that's the way I want it,' he added grimly.

Danny gave him a sharp look, but his expression was unreadable. 'Please don't dissolve your business deal because of me,' she pleaded with him softly. 'I was a bit too hot-headed.' And she had never felt so damned stupid in her life, just wanted to get away from this nightmare. And she never ran from a situation.

His eyes narrowed on Paul Banyon. 'Is that the truth?'

'I may have been a little too familiar——'

'It was only harmless flirtation——'

'How much of a flirtation?' Pierce cut in on her defence of the other man.

'It was nothing——'

'I let her know I'd like to sleep with her,' Paul told him calmly. 'I had no idea she was important to you.'

'And now that you do?' Pierce grated icily.

The other man shrugged. 'I will, of course, treat her as a friend, and nothing more than that. Damn it, Sutherland, I don't cut in on other people's relationships.'

Danny couldn't believe she was the cause of this scene; Pierce must think her a complete fool. As well as a nuisance. 'I—er—I have to go,' she said awkwardly. 'I've—er—I've left the coffee percolator on,' she invented desperately.

'Does that matter?' Clarissa looked confused by the statement.

'Shut up, Clarissa,' her father ordered wearily.

'But——'

'Are we staying or leaving, Pierce?' Paul asked

impatiently. 'If we're staying we could go to our rooms and give you some privacy.'

'That isn't necessary.' Danny hurried to the door. 'I'm so sorry,' she said again before running out into the night, the two dogs running along with her.

Oh, she was so clever, she had *known* Pierce wanted her! She had made a complete fool of herself—and Pierce. She doubted he would ever forgive her. She doubted *she* would ever forgive herself!

She had been expecting the knock on the back door ever since she returned home ten minutes earlier, her face full of misery as she opened the door to look out at Pierce. 'Can you ever forgive me?' she groaned, swallowing hard. 'I didn't know you had guests, and then when I did I——' Pierce cut her off by pulling her into his arms, his kiss gentle. 'Oh, Pierce!' she moaned shakily, burying her face in his chest. 'Did the Banyons leave?'

'No, they're staying the night, as planned.' He kissed the top of her head, his hands moving restlessly over her back. 'And our business deal will go through as planned, too.'

She looked up at him. 'Then shouldn't you be back at the house with them?'

He shook his head, his eyes a warm blue-grey. 'They don't need me to get to sleep.'

'But——'

'Danielle, I'm staying here with you tonight,' he interrupted firmly. 'And every other night.'

'Aren't you angry with me for bursting in on you the way I did?' she frowned.

'No.' His mouth quirked. 'I was quite impressed, especially once I realised you had come to get me and then decided to save me from the clutches of the sweet Clarissa.'

'How on earth did a man like Paul Banyon raise such a daughter?' she derided.

'I have no idea—and I'm not really interested,' he added firmly. 'I'm not interested in anything but you at this moment. I missed you today,' he told her raggedly.

'Surely my greeting tonight was beyond expectations?' she said with self-disgust.

Pierce began to chuckle. 'It was spectacular. Although it might have been more impressive if you had come in wearing a leopard-skin bikini, looking like Jane of the Jungle! On second thoughts, perhaps not,' he rasped grimly. 'No man needs that sort of stimulation when looking at you!'

'Jealous, Pierce?' She expressed surprise.

'Intensely.' He nodded.

She put her hand in to his. 'Let's go to bed, hm?'

'Benson is standing outside again,' he warned, his eyes hard.

'I don't care.' She shook her head, already knowing he wouldn't break that particular rule for her.

'I called New York again today,' he revealed abruptly. 'Nigel and Cheryl will be back tomorrow; I've invited the two of them down here for the night.'

'Oh.'

'You don't sound too happy about it.' He frowned.

She grimaced. 'I just don't want Cheryl to get the idea I'm spying on her—even if I am!'

'It's worrying you, Danielle,' he said tersely. 'And that's rather silly when you and Cheryl could sort all this out with a brief conversation.'

'You're right,' she agreed with a sigh. 'I know you are. I just won't know what to say to Cheryl.'

'I think your sister is the one who should do the talking—don't you?'

'I suppose so,' she agreed, nodding slowly. 'Although she isn't going to like it.'

'Well, as she's over eighteen and perfectly free to do what she wants I have to sympathise with her on that. But I don't approve of her worrying you,' he added darkly.

'She probably doesn't even realise she has,' Danny realised ruefully.

'Let's not talk about them any more tonight?' Pierce encouraged throatily.

No, tonight, as last night, was theirs.

CHAPTER SIX

IT seemed idiotic to feel nervous about seeing your own sister, and yet she was. She and Cheryl seemed to have grown apart lately, what other reason could Cheryl have for going to New York with Nigel Patrick without telling anyone; her sister must have realised the family would worry when they couldn't reach her on the telephone. Danny had had her distraught mother on the telephone only this morning, concerned because Cheryl hadn't answered any of her calls. It hadn't been easy convincing her mother that there was nothing to worry about.

Pierce had sent the helicopter to collect Cheryl and Nigel from the airport, and Danny was waiting in his lounge for them now, Pierce called away to an urgent telephone call. And Danny still had no idea what to say to Cheryl, or even if her sister was aware she was going to be here today.

It had been a hectic day so far, spending part of the morning with Pierce as he entertained Paul and Clarissa Banyon, the older man's easy charm erasing any awkwardness that might have occurred from the evening before.

'Calm down,' Pierce urged softly as he came back into the room, coming up behind her to nuzzle into her throat.

'I can't help it.' She turned into his arms.

'Cheryl has always been impulsive, but this time she seems to have gone too far.'

'She's old enough to know her own mind.'

'You've never met her,' Danny warned. 'She's very young for her age in some ways, and your nephew is thirty.'

'I think your sister might retaliate to that accusation by pointing out that the age difference between us is a lot more than that,' he said drily.

'That's different.'

'That's probably the way Cheryl feels about Nigel,' Pierce warned.

Danny sighed. 'If she's really happy with Nigel then it's her decision.'

'You don't sound very sure,' he teased lightly.

'It's her lack of total commitment to either Gary or Nigel that bothers me,' she admitted. 'I don't think she really knows what she wants.'

'Probably not,' Pierce drawled. 'But you can be sure that if Nigel wants her he'll be doing a very good job of convincing her he's what she wants!'

'As forceful and determined as his uncle, hm?' she mocked.

'I like to think of myself as persuasive,' he murmured against her throat.

For the next few minutes he attempted to 'persuade' her that they had time to go back to his bedroom before their guests arrived, only the sound of the helicopter preventing her from *being* persuaded.

'They're here,' she gasped nervously, smoothing skirt to her lemon sun-dress, checking the appearance of her hair, and then chastising herself for being nervous in the first place; Cheryl was her sister, for goodness' sake.

'Obviously,' Pierce mocked indulgently.

She stood at his side as they waited for the other couple, hardly able to believe the glowingly beautiful woman with the tall handsome man was her sister Cheryl. She had never seen her sister look so beautiful, her hazel eyes glowing. Her blonde hair had been restyled, the same length as Danny's now, the more sophisticated style suiting her, the cream silk dress she was wearing obviously a designer model.

'Danny!' she cried excitedly, running across the room to hug her. 'I had no idea you were going to be here.' She turned back to Nigel. 'Was it a surprise?'

He looked at Danny with steady blue eyes, a young version of Pierce, tall and dark, with a lithe athletic body. 'For both of us,' he drawled cryptically, looking at his uncle consideringly.

Cheryl looked shyly at Pierce, too. 'It's nice to meet you at last.'

'I've been looking forward to this moment, too,' he assured her softly.

'Pierce?' Nigel prompted warily.

He turned to the younger man with steely eyes. 'I suggest we go and see to the organisation of your luggage while Danielle and Cheryl make their proper greetings.'

Nigel strode across the room to kiss Cheryl lingeringly on the mouth. 'I shouldn't be long.'

'I'm sure Cheryl will survive without you for the few minutes we'll be gone,' Pierce mocked in a hard voice.

'Possibly,' his nephew snapped, following him out the room. 'But will I?'

'Isn't he wonderful!' Cheryl clasped Danny's hands excitedly. 'I love him so much.'

'Cheryl . . .'

'Are you and Pierce Sutherland—friends?' her sister probed interestedly.

'What on earth made you ask that?' she asked warily.

'The way he said your name,' Cheryl laughed. 'It was *so* sexy.'

'Cheryl . . .'

'Of course he's not as sexy as Nigel,' her sister chattered lightly. 'But he is a very handsome man. *Are* you involved with him?'

'Don't you think you should be the one answering that question—about Nigel,' Danny cut in irritably. 'You disappear to New York for five days with a man none of your family even know, miss university as if it's unimportant to you, and then come back and start questioning *me*!'

'You've met Nigel before,' Cheryl snapped. 'And I've finished all my exams, so missing the last week doesn't really matter. As for New York . . .'

'Oh, I'm so glad you remembered New York!' she said with sarcasm.

'Stop acting like a maiden aunt instead of my sister,' Cheryl dismissed impatiently.

'I *feel* like your maiden aunt,' she assured her exasperatedly. 'Mum and Dad have been worried sick——'

'I called them from the airport——'

'That's something at least. Don't you think——'

'Danny, before you say anything else I think I should tell you that Nigel and I were married the morning we left for New York,' Cheryl cut in quietly.

She swallowed hard, all the breath seeming to be knocked from her body. Married? Her little sister was married! She looked in disbelief at the platinum wedding ring Cheryl proudly displayed, sure she must have made some words of admiration by the glow of pleasure in her sister's face.

'Nigel wanted to buy me an engagement ring while we were in New York,' Cheryl chatted on, 'but I don't want one, I've had one engagement; it didn't work out.'

'Gary?'

'Has been an absolute dear.' Cheryl nodded.

'He knows?' she gasped.

'I told him last weekend when he came up to London that I couldn't marry him.'

'But he—he came round at the beginning of the week,' Danny stuttered. 'He didn't say a word to me then.'

Cheryl smiled. 'I told you he's been a dear.'

'But ... he spoke of you as if nothing had happened.' Danny frowned.

Her sister nodded. 'I'm sure as far as he's concerned nothing really has. Sometimes it happens this way, you grow up and become friends instead of lovers. I'm sure we'll always remain friends, and although you have to like the person you marry you can't marry the person who is just a good friend.'

'Cheryl, are you absolutely sure he understood what you were telling him?' She couldn't believe Gary could act so—so undisturbed.

Cheryl shrugged. 'I gave him back his ring.'

'And he didn't think you were asking him to get it cleaned or something?'

'Danny,' her sister said patiently, 'I explained to him about Nigel, told him that I intended marrying him if he asked me, *then* I gave Gary back his ring. He couldn't have misunderstood that!'

No, he couldn't. And yet he had seemed to be unaffected by it. 'He wasn't upset?' she persisted.

'He was disappointed,' her sister corrected.

'But *you* were so jealous because I'd had him to the house for dinner!'

Cheryl's mouth quirked. 'Wasn't I supposed to be?'

'You mean you were having me on?'

'You weren't very subtle, Danny,' she teased, giggling a little. 'Even dear sweet Gary guessed what you were up to!'

'Oh, that's just marvellous!' she said in disgust.

Cheryl sobered. 'We both know you meant well, Danny. But Gary admitted that he had known things weren't right between us for the last six months or so—before I had even met Nigel,' she added pointedly. 'Gary just didn't want to hurt my feelings by saying so.' She shrugged.

'And your marriage to Nigel?'

Cheryl's expression turned to one of extreme tenderness. 'I've never felt so happy,' she smiled. 'When he got back Sunday evening he asked me to marry him, and when I accepted he told me he had been walking about with a marriage licence in his pocket since the day after we met, just hoping I would say yes. How could I resist him after that! It was too irresistible not to get married before we went to New York.'

She could see that her sister was happy with her new husband, she just didn't see why they needed to get married so quickly.

'You would all have tried to talk me out of it,' Cheryl defended when she said so. 'I didn't want to wait, and neither did Nigel.' She blushed. 'We were tired of waiting.'

'I am pleased for you, but I just——'

'No buts, Danny,' she encouraged. 'Just be happy for me. And it looks as if you won't have lost out on your opportunity to be my bridesmaid either,' she grimaced. 'Mum and Dad are insisting we have a second wedding in church.'

'How does Nigel feel about that?' she derided. 'Most men try to avoid even *one* wedding!'

Cheryl laughed happily. 'Now that we've acted so impulsively it's time to please the in-laws,' she teased. 'We met Nigel's parents while we were away, and I think they would like us to have a grander wedding, too. Nigel would like Pierce to be his best man.'

Danny frowned. 'Did he know that the two of you were married?'

'No one did.' Cheryl shook her head. 'We were having too good a time to spoil it. Now tell me about you and Pierce. And don't say there's nothing going on, even a child could see that there is.'

And her sister was far from being that, she had learnt today. Cheryl was much more mature than she had given her credit for, and she had no doubt that this new Cheryl would make a success of her marriage.

'I love him,' she replied with complete candour. 'And he wants me.'

'And?'

'And he's got me.'

Her sister nodded. 'You know he was married?'

'Yes,' she sighed. 'But it was so long ago, and one unhappy marriage . . .'

'Oh, it wasn't unhappy,' Cheryl instantly denied with a frown. 'They were both very young, but from what Nigel's told me the two of them were ecstatically happy together.'

She had assumed, from the little Pierce had told her, that he had loved his wife and the emotion hadn't been reciprocated. But if they had been so happy together, why was Pierce so bitter about the past? It was just something else to add to the list of things she didn't know about the man she loved.

'Danny——'

'Danielle, there's something you should know,' Pierce strode back into the room, quickly followed by Nigel, the younger man putting his arm protectively about Cheryl's waist. 'Cheryl and Nigel——'

'Are married,' she finished self-derisively, moving to kiss her new brother-in-law on the cheek. 'Welcome to the family,' she said ruefully.

Cheryl kissed Pierce. 'I don't think I can bring myself to call you "uncle"—in the circumstances.'

Her eyes glowed with mischief as she looked from Danny pointedly back to Pierce.

His mouth quirked mockingly. 'In the circumstances,' he drawled, 'maybe you're right.'

'Circumstances?' Only Nigel still looked puzzled. 'What circumstances?'

'Come with me while I freshen up and change, darling,' Cheryl invited. 'And I'll tell you.'

Danny stood at Pierce's side as the other couple left the room, Nigel still frowning as Cheryl refused to answer him.

'What have you been telling your sister about us?' Pierce asked drily.

'Only that I love you,' she replied distractedly, still preoccupied with the fact that Pierce's marriage had been a happy one. And his memories, obviously good ones, were almost as old as she was! 'She guessed the rest,' Danny dismissed.

'What are your feelings about them being married?'

'I'm sure they will be very happy together.'

He nodded. 'They're driving down to see your parents tomorrow.'

'Mum and Dad will like that.'

'Why don't you go with them?'

She raised startled eyes. 'You——'

'No, not me,' he replied harshly. 'But I understand this is a family time, that you might like to join in the celebrations.'

'You're part of Nigel's family,' she pointed out softly.

'And I'll celebrate with him today,' Pierce rasped dismissively.

'Then so will I.'

'I'd rather you went with them tomorrow,' he told her abruptly.

'Why?' she looked up curiously at his closed expression.

'I have someone coming here to see me tomorrow——'

'Oh—oh, I see.' She paled, turning away. 'In that case——'

'You don't *see* at all, Danielle,' Pierce roughly jerked up her chin so that he could look at her face. 'My visitor tomorrow is a man. He and I have business together.'

'And you would prefer it if I weren't around,' she realised heavily. 'I apologised for yesterday; I can assure you I'll never do anything like that again. It was only——'

'Danielle, I told you, I found your entrance last night spectacular—and so did Paul.' He grasped her shoulders. 'But this meeting tomorrow is very important to me. It is also extremely private.'

She also knew that he didn't want to become any more involved with her family than he already was, that it was all part of avoiding any deep relationship. 'I'll go with Cheryl and Nigel,' she decided. 'I haven't seen my parents for some time, and——'

'You'll be back tomorrow night?' He frowned.

She smiled warmly. 'If you want me to be.'

'I do.' He nodded abruptly, adding nothing to the statement.

She nodded. 'Then I'll be back.'

'Would you like to "freshen up and change" before we eat?' he suggested softly.

'Aren't you ever satisfied?' she teased.

'Of you?' He raised dark brows, as if he were slightly surprised by the answer. 'No.'

They still arrived back downstairs for aperitifs before the newly married couple. Dinner was a light-hearted affair, even Pierce relaxed a little under the glow of Cheryl's obvious happiness. Nigel looked only slightly less radiant than his wife, apparently ignoring the relationship Cheryl must have told him existed between his uncle and Danny.

That assumption was quickly dispelled!

Nigel joined Danny out on the terrace as Cheryl and Pierce decided what music they were to listen to. He stood silently at her side for several minutes, gazing up at the moonlight. Finally he spoke. 'I've never seen Pierce this relaxed.'

Danny turned to smile at him. 'It's been a successful evening.'

'I didn't just mean tonight.' Nigel shook his head. 'He's seemed more at ease when I've spoken to him on the telephone this last week.'

'I hadn't noticed.' But she had, knew every subtle change in the man she loved. And there was something about his business meeting tomorrow that made her uneasy. Who had business meetings on a Sunday? Extremely private, Pierce had said. Her uneasiness about the situation was hard to describe, but it existed.

'He seems to have put it out of his mind for a while,' Nigel added thoughtfully.

Danny gave him a sharp look. 'Put what out of his mind?'

'For sixteen years he's been eaten up by guilt and remorse, it's time he put it all behind him and started to live normally again.'

Sixteen years? Why on earth should Pierce feel guilt and remorse about his wife's death? Nigel seemed to assume she knew. Maybe she would have known if she hadn't been five years old at the time! And she wasn't about to ask Pierce himself, knew he would resent the intrusion into his privacy.

'Cheryl says you're in love with him.' Nigel looked at her intently. 'If you are, then get him to give up. It's been sixteen years now, he has to let go.'

'I'm sorry, Nigel, but I——'

'I hope to God you aren't encouraging him in the insanity,' he rasped. 'It's self-destructive!'

'I——'

'Come on, you two,' Cheryl teased lightly as she stood in the doorway. 'Pierce has made room for us to dance.'

'Have you been charming my taciturn uncle?' Nigel mockingly reproved his wife.

'I've been charming her.' Pierce joined Cheryl. 'She's promised me the first dance.'

Pierce listened with indulgent amusement as Cheryl chattered to him while they danced, Nigel watched them with indulgence as he danced with Danny.

'I'll take care of her.' Nigel suddenly noticed Danny's serious expression. 'She's very special to me.'

That hadn't been the reason for her brooding thoughts, genuinely concerned about Nigel's enigmatic conversation about Pierce. She shook off her feelings of apprehension with effort, smiling brightly. 'She seems to think you're special too,' she challenged.

'That's because I am,' he returned cheekily.

Danny gave a splutter of laughter. 'Modest, too. My parents are going to love you!' She knew her father would like his outspoken wit, her mother his air of confidence and caring.

'I hope so.' He looked slightly disconcerted. 'It's very important to Cheryl that they do, and if it's important to her then it's important to me, too.'

Danny gave his shoulder a reassuring squeeze. 'Believe me, they always wanted a son like you. I hope you don't mind,' she frowned, 'but I'd like to go with you tomorrow.'

'Pierce?'

Her gaze was suddenly evasive. 'He has an important business meeting.'

Nigel frowned. 'You don't happen to know who with, do you?'

'He didn't say.' She shrugged lightly. 'It could be Paul Banyon.'

'He and Clarissa are already on their way back to the States.' Nigel shook his head. 'Damn,' he muttered grimly. 'When will he stop tormenting himself in this way!'

'Nigel?'

'Cheryl would like to dance with her husband now,' Pierce cut in lightly, although there was steel in his eyes.

Danny could feel the tension in him as they danced to the romantic music, guessed that he had probably overheard part of her conversation with Nigel. And he didn't like it. 'Pierce, I——'

'I don't care to be discussed with my nephew in that way,' he cut in icily. 'And if you intend to continue to gossip in this way I believe our relationship will have to end.'

Danny gasped at the inflexibility in his voice. 'I wasn't gossiping!'

'You told Nigel of my meeting tomorrow when it is none of his business!'

'I thought he would already know——'

'I told you, it's a private meeting!'

'You also said it was business,' she reminded exasperatedly.

'As my accountant, Nigel is not told of all my business meetings,' Pierce dismissed haughtily.

'Well, I'm sorry.'

'Your apology is accepted.' He nodded distantly, ignoring her angry snort at his interrupting of her sarcasm. 'Now I believe it's time to politely end this evening; Cheryl looks very tired.'

Cheryl was yawning as she and Nigel went upstairs to their suite, the atmosphere suddenly very tense in the lounge. Danny stood awkwardly in the middle of the room as Pierce poured himself a drink when she refused his offer.

'Where do you want to sleep tonight?' he suddenly asked abruptly.

She didn't know if the query were a genuine one or a way of asking *if* they would be sharing a bed tonight. 'It's cosier in my bed,' she answered softly.

'Cosier?' He derided the description. These black moods of sarcasm and coldness were becoming less frequent, but they were all the more cutting because of that.

'I realise my bed isn't long enough for you,' she lightly teased. 'But at least we can't lose each other in it.' She found his king-size bed *too* large!

'Then let's go.' He threw the drink to the back of his throat before leaving the empty glass on the table.

Their lovemaking was different again that night. Pierce didn't want her to reciprocate the caresses he had taught her, although he sent her over the edge of desire time and time again, taking her with deliberate slowness. It was as if he were punishing her for something, and afterwards Danny lay unfulfilled emotionally, but physically satiated, in his arms.

As she had known they would, her parents approved of their new son-in-law, Danny coming in for a few 'old maid' jokes because her younger sister had married before her. It was a light-hearted day, full of laughter and shared happiness. And Danny couldn't stop thinking about Pierce, wondering who he was seeing today.

They had parted stiltedly this morning, and she couldn't help wondering if part of that was because he found their relationship, a constant relationship that he had claimed he didn't want, too claustrophobic for him after years of transient affairs.

'You're very quiet?' Nigel prompted softly on the drive home; the last two days of travelling had finally taken their toll on Cheryl, as she slept at his side.

She sighed. 'About the conversation we didn't get to finish last night . . .'

'I'm not allowed to finish it, I'm afraid.' He grimaced.

Danny frowned at his choice of words. 'Not allowed?'

'Pierce's orders.' He nodded regretfully. 'And, believe me, when he issues that type of order you obey!'

She drew in a ragged breath. 'He spoke to you this morning before we left?'

'Very succinctly.' Nigel pulled a face. 'Apparently I've been talking out of turn.'

'About his wife?'

'Yes.'

She sighed. 'He won't allow anyone to talk about her, will he, not even himself.'

'Sally was a very beautiful woman, inside and out,' he told her softly. 'And her death is a matter of public record. I have a childhood memory of fiery green eyes, black gypsy-like hair, and a smiling, laughing face.'

Danny sighed again. 'Her memory sounds too much competition for any woman.'

'Pierce needs you,' Nigel insisted huskily. 'He just doesn't think he does,' he added derisively.

She gave a soft laugh. 'You're very encouraging, brother-in-law.'

'Cheryl and I have been thinking of making you an aunty,' he announced conversationally.

'Already?' she gasped.

Nigel shrugged. 'Why not? Cheryl loves children, and I'm not getting any younger.'

It was exhilarating to see how happy her sister

and this man were, and Danny felt her own spirits lift a little, feeling the anticipation of seeing Pierce again as they neared the estate; the happy couple were to leave her there before they drove on to London.

'Mr Sutherland told me to inform you he's expecting you at the house,' Dave Benson told her as soon as she entered the grounds.

When they had parted that morning, it was without making any arrangements to meet in the evening, and she could only hope his mood had mellowed during the day. He was waiting for her in the lounge.

'I was hoping you wouldn't be too late getting back,' he said briskly, giving her no greeting. 'I have to fly to London tonight . . .'

'Oh, no!' Her protest was instinctive, and she knew by the narrowing of icy eyes that it was unwelcome.

'. . . before flying on to Washington, D.C. tomorrow,' he finished in a steely voice.

She knew that yesterday there had been no such plans, that the visitor he had had today must have prompted such action. And that it also had something to do with his dead wife. 'Let me come with you,' she said impulsively. 'I'm due for a holiday,' she added at his suddenly wary expression.

'This will be a business trip for me,' he told her abruptly. 'And I never take women with me on business trips,' he bit out hardily.

'You had a woman with you in Paris.'

'I didn't take her with me, and that wasn't a business trip.'

'I wouldn't get in the way,' she pleaded. 'And

I've never been to Washington.' She had never been anywhere farther than France, and Washington certainly wasn't the place that had most appealed to her if she ever did get to go to America. But somehow she sensed it was imperative she accompany him, that he might need her.

'I have several—business meetings, to attend,' Pierce rasped. 'What would you do with yourself all day?'

She sensed he was weakening and she pushed ahead while she could. 'You wouldn't be working all the time, and we could be together the times you aren't. I've always wanted to spend a holiday in a Washington hotel bedroom!'

Pierce chuckled. 'If you can be ready to leave in half an hour you just might do that.'

'I'll be ready,' she promised instantly, hurrying to the door, sure that this trip to Washington would solve at least part of the puzzle about Pierce's wife.

CHAPTER SEVEN

FLYING on the Concorde was an experience in itself, Danny enthralled by the way they were travelling so high in the sky they could see the curvature of the earth, Pierce uninterested in his surroundings as he sat back in his seat with his eyes closed.

In fact, Danny had been impressed at the whole VIP treatment they had received, including the delivery of her passport with its visa minutes before their plane departed.

She had been surprised to learn they were travelling on a public plane, knowing Pierce owned his own jet. But he had told her that the difference in flight time more than made up for that fact. That he had acquired all the seats in this section of the plane, only half a dozen of his bodyguards seated with them, meant that he still maintained complete privacy.

Danny found it all a little strange, like being wrapped in a cocoon of cottonwool, but if this was the way Pierce usually travelled then who was she to question it. Their stopover in London had been the same, guards outside their suite all night, several of them actually inside. It had made things a little awkward, especially when it came time to go to bed, and she could understand why Pierce usually made these trips without a woman present.

From Dulles airport Pierce's party was driven

in to Washington by three long black limousines, Don Bridgeman dealing with the hotel reception before they arrived at The Hilton Towers, their suite thoroughly searched, security guards once more outside the doors, two more in one of the bedrooms, the door to this room closed as Danny and Pierce sat together in the lounge.

'Is it always like this?' she asked casually, gazing down on to the garden, people around the pool in the humid heat of the day. She hadn't known what to expect of the Washington weather, but the humidity had come as something of a shock to her, and she had removed the jacket to her beige linen suit as soon as they had left the airport, her blouse sticking to her back within seconds.

'Like what?'

She could tell he was genuinely puzzled by the question. 'Don't you ever wish you could just have some privacy?'

His mouth twisted. 'I get that back at the house. In places like this I'd rather take precautions against some nut walking into the room and shooting me just because I have more money than he does.'

'In Washington D.C.?'

'Anywhere,' he said pointedly. 'No one wishes more than I do that the world were a safer place, but it isn't, and only a fool takes chances.'

She forced a bright smile. 'This is a wonderful hotel, isn't it,' she said lightly. 'Have you stayed here before?'

'More times than I can remember.' He nodded abruptly.

She had found it very intriguing the way they had gone up in the lift to The Hilton Towers, this part of the hotel almost separate from the actual Hilton Hotel downstairs, even a separate receptionist at a desk to greet them as they stepped out of the lift. But obviously Pierce wasn't as impressed by the surrounding opulence as she was.

'Can we go down to the pool later?'

'No,' he answered coldly.

'But I'm hot and sticky——'

'Then take a shower.' He shrugged.

'Pierce?'

'If this is an example of your "not getting in the way",' he stood up forcefully, 'it isn't good enough. I can certainly do without hearing your whining complaints!' he snapped savagely.

He was deliberately trying to wound—and he was succeeding, no softening to his granite-like features even though he could see he had hurt her. 'I think I'll go and unpack,' she told him lightly.

'Danielle. . .?' He halted her at the bedroom door.

'Yes?'

'Could the unpacking wait a while?'

She turned to face him, seeing the desire in his eyes. 'No,' she answered curtly, too upset to respond to the invitation. 'I don't think it can.'

She had decided at the beginning of their relationship that she would only take what he wanted to give, but she wouldn't be treated as a sex object, only accepted as his equal in his bed. His other women may have become accustomed to it, but she never would.

She had no idea what Pierce did while she unpacked, but rather deliberately kept her mind blank as she worked, lying down on the bed once she had finished, reluctant to join Pierce.

It was dark in the room when she woke, although she realised this was mainly due to the curtains being pulled at the windows, that it was still light outside.

It seemed Pierce must have pulled the curtains because she had also been undressed before being put under the covers, the air-conditioning keeping the room cool. She was grateful for his thoughtfulness, knowing that the linen skirt to her suit would have been very badly creased if she had slept in it.

'Awake?'

She turned over at the husky query, Pierce was lying on the bed at her side wearing only a robe, his hair looking slightly damp from the shower he must have taken.

'You look better.' He smoothed the hair from her eyes. 'You looked a little pale earlier.'

She looked up at him with her heart in her eyes. 'I'm sorry if I was a nag before.'

'You weren't, and you know it,' he sighed. 'I'm not used to living in this close proximity with a woman, especially one I actually like,' he added with self-disgust. 'Living with you is showing me just how selfish I've become over the years.'

'Not selfish.' She shook her head. 'Just independent of people.'

'Selfish, and damned arrogant,' he rasped, bending to kiss her lightly on the lips. 'Order yourself some dinner, I'll be back later.'

She sat up as he threw off his robe to begin dressing. 'You're going out now?'

He nodded, selecting the clothes he was going to wear. 'I shouldn't be more than an hour or two.'

It was a strange time of day for a business meeting, but she was slowly learning to silence her impetuous tongue. 'Maybe I should just wait here for you,' she teased, pleased when the frown left his brow and he smiled.

'Maybe you had better eat so that you have the strength for what I have in mind for later,' he drawled, pulling on a beige lightweight jacket to contrast with the brown trousers and oatmeal shirt he wore. 'But dress first, hm?' he chuckled wryly. 'I'm leaving Dawson and Redman in the suite.' He bent down to kiss the bared part of her breasts. 'And your body is for my delectation only,' he added sternly.

She put her arms up about his neck. 'I promise not to do a streak through the suite. But I'll miss you,' she told him seriously.

'Keep that thought in mind.' He straightened with a smile. 'And I'll collect on it later.'

Danny didn't particularly enjoy the solitary dinner she ordered in the suite. She was unable to persuade Peter Redman or Bob Dawson to join her, although Peter accepted her invitation to join her for a stroll round the shop downstairs in the hotel, where she found quite an assortment of goods in the shops, from sweets to expensive jewellery—*very* expensive jewellery!

Pierce still hadn't come back by the time they returned upstairs, and so she invited the two men to a game of cards, having switched on the television while she ate her dinner and found the programmes as boring as the English ones were this time of year, all repeats of the previous season.

'I don't think Mr Sutherland would approve of us playing for money.' Bob frowned, a small man with a balding head, the muscles bulging beneath his shirt giving lie to his initial weak appearance.

'Neither do I,' she laughed. 'But it's boring if you don't play for something. How about matchsticks?'

None of them smoked, and so Danny ended up ripping the cardboard matches from the complimentary match-books that had been left out in the ashtrays.

It was an uproarious game of poker, the two men allowing for her inexperience before they realised she was far from being a novice, winning every hand.

'We had a lot of spare time between classes at college, and what else could I do with twenty-five men?' she said with feigned coyness.

'What indeed?' Peter drawled—he was in his late twenties.

'Peter!' Bob warned softly.

'Sorry,' the younger man muttered. 'I didn't mean to be rude, Dan—er, Miss Martin——'

'You never call me Miss Martin,' she derided.

'No. Well—I——'

'I'm Danny, Peter,' she encouraged. 'I was before Pierce and I became friends, and I will be afterwards too.'

'Afterwards?'

Her mouth twisted. 'I'm sure you must be

more aware than I am of the short life of such relationships for Pierce.'

He looked uncomfortable about the fact. 'Yes. But——'

'I'm the same as all the others, Peter,' she assured him gently. 'I'm just a little more pushy.'

'I don't know, some of them——'

'Peter, learn a little discretion,' Bob told him impatiently. 'Danny doesn't want to hear about them.'

No, she didn't, not even for curiosity's sake. 'I just don't want you to start treating me any differently,' she said softly. 'When I'm no longer with Pierce I'll still be working on the estate.'

'Won't you find that——'

'Peter, for God's sake!' the older man reproved exasperatedly. 'I'm sorry about this, Danny.' He grimaced. 'Some people have no tact.' He glared at the younger man.

Danny laughed, not in the least offended, knowing Peter was just curious, as Bob must be, although he was too polite to show it. 'That makes two of us.' She put down her cards. 'A straight flush!'

'You're too good for us.' Bob pushed the pile of matches from the middle of the table to join the substantial amount she had already amassed throughout the game.

'Want to stop?' She quirked her brows mockingly.

'Certainly not,' he grinned. 'I intend winning some of my matches back!'

For the next two hours the matches moved

backwards and forwards across the table—and Danny's concentration grew less and less. A business meeting shouldn't take as long as this; Pierce must have been out at least four hours. But he had taken Don Bridgeman and Jerry Adams with him, so he must be all right. She knew him well enough to know he wouldn't have gone to see another woman, so what was keeping him?

'Mine, I believe.' Peter collected his winnings with a triumphant smile.

'This all looks very cosy,' Pierce rasped harshly.

Danny's face lit up as she turned to see him standing just inside the room, running into his arms, uncaring of his unyielding expression as she pressed her face against his chest. 'I've been worried about you,' she told him huskily.

'It looks like it!' He looked pointedly over at the table she had just left.

Danny suddenly saw what he must see, the cards and three glasses of beer on the table, and she began to giggle. The room looked like a gambling den!

Pierce gave her a fierce look. 'I'm glad you can see something funny about this.' His cold gaze raked over the two men who had jumped to their feet at the first sound of his voice. 'I asked you to look after her,' he bit out. 'Not include her in your poker game!'

Both men remained silent, and Danny knew they weren't going to defend themselves at the risk of getting her into more trouble. 'Er—Pierce . . .'

'Not that I suppose you're completely innocent,' he added disgustedly. 'Trouble seems to follow you about!'

'It was *my* poker game.' She grimaced.

'*What?*'

'Well, I was bored, and——'

'You can go now,' he dismissed the two men wearily. 'I should have guessed the poker was Danny's idea; I hope you didn't lose too much.'

'Forty-eight for Peter, and thirty-two for Bob,' she drawled once they were alone.

'You took their money off them?' Pierce sounded disbelieving.

She shook her head. 'Matchsticks,' she teased. 'Did your meeting go okay?'

'Yes.' He threw off his jacket, pouring himself a glass of whisky while Danny cleared the table. 'I didn't mean to be gone so long.'

'You're back now,' she smiled, the room once more returned to order.

'I bought you a present.' He searched through the breast pocket of his jacket.

'For me?' she said excitedly, her expression suddenly wary as he took out a square, flat jewellery case. She usually received flowers or chocolates from the men she had dated in the past, this looked as if it were something much more expensive than that.

'I noticed you have pierced ears, so . . .' Pierce flicked open the case to reveal a diamond pendant the size of a penny, with matching droplet earrings.

Danny gasped at the exquisite beauty of the jewellery, shaking her head as she made no attempt to touch the gleaming stones. She had seen the set of expensive jewellery downstairs in the shop, and the price-ticket that had been on it made her head spin.

'I realise you couldn't wear them while you're working,' Pierce derided. 'But——'

'I couldn't wear them at all.' She looked up at him with pained eyes. 'Putting me in my place, Pierce?'

He blinked. 'What the hell are you talking about?'

'I don't want the jewellery from you, I have no *price*!' She glared at him.

He recoiled as if she had hit him, the diamond earring he held slipping from his fingers back into the case. 'They were a gift, Danielle,' he said dully. 'Not payments for any services you may have given!'

'Do you know the difference?' she snapped.

'Do you?'

She paled at the pain in his voice. 'Pierce——'

'Danielle, no matter what you believe, they were a gift. I thought how beautiful they would look against your hair, and I imagined the pendant nestled between your breasts, the way I like to be when we sleep.' His voice was harsh now. 'Gratitude might have had something to do with it,' he nodded grimly. 'But for the honesty you always give me, not for your body.'

She had sadly misjudged the situation, had badly hurt his feelings. 'Pierce, I'm sorry,' she looked at him pleadingly. 'I just thought—I think too much!' she groaned awkwardly. 'And I'm not doing a very good job of it. Do you think the management would mind if I brought a lawn-mower up here?'

His expression lightened at her feeble attempt to lessen the tension. 'I think they might. Can't you think any other way?'

'Swimming in a pool? No, that's you,' she dismissed. 'Nope, it's the mower or nothing,' she derided.

Pierce took her in his arms. 'For what I have in mind for the next hour or so you don't need to think at all,' he murmured.

'Oh?' She pretended puzzlement.

'I have a yearning to see you in the necklace and earrings,' he spoke softly against her throat. '*Just* the necklace and earrings.'

Danny chuckled appreciatively, sensing the moment of danger was over. 'How deliciously erotic, Mr Sutherland.'

'That's what I thought.' He smiled down at her. 'The assistant downstairs would have been most shocked if she had known what I was thinking as I purchased the jewellery.'

'And you think I'm not!' She feigned indignation.

'I know you aren't,' Pierce chuckled. 'When it comes to making love you're unshockable!'

Although he tried to shock her through the hours of the night, coming to her again and again with a shared pleasure. And as they rested in each other's arms between those times Danny could only cling to him, glad that the near-disaster she had made of the evening had been averted. Pierce was a man who needed to give materially, simply because he couldn't feel love. The gift of the jewellery was his only way of showing emotion. And she had so nearly thrown it back in his face. The necklace and earrings were far too expensive for her to keep, but she would give them back when—when she had to let Pierce go.

'Darling?' he queried huskily as her arms tightened about him instinctively.

'Just a bad dream.' She smiled down at him reassuringly as he rested against her breasts.

'Sure?' He frowned.

'Yes.' She nodded, knowing that she was searching for a dream, although not a bad one. It was one where she and Pierce remained together always; an impossible dream. 'I think I'm feeling neglected,' she pouted.

'Neglected!' he snorted disbelievingly.

'Very,' she said in a hurt voice, her eyes twinkling with mischief. 'Isn't jet-lag wonderful; you feel wide awake when you should be sleeping and sleepy when you should be awake! I'd like to stay awake all night and sleep all day tomorrow.'

Pierce grimaced as he leant up on his elbow. 'You're the first person I've ever heard call jet-lag wonderful,' he derided. 'And besides, you aren't supposed to feel jet-lag after travelling on Concorde.'

'Then why am I awake when I should be asleep?' Danny frowned.

'Because you're feeling neglected.' He nuzzled her throat with firm lips. 'I'll soon remedy that.'

She found the 'remedy' quite exhausting, falling into a deep sleep in his arms afterwards, the rigours of the day finally catching up with her.

Pierce was in the shower when she woke next morning, and she lay back on the pillows as she waited for him to come back.

He was wearing only black trousers when he emerged from the bathroom, rubbing his hair dry with a towel. 'Good morning,' he greeted indulgently.

She smiled. 'I told you I was awake when I should be sleepy, and vice versa.'

'What was the dream, Danielle?' He frowned.

He would become withdrawn again if she told him it was losing him! 'I can't remember,' she dismissed, holding out her arms to him.

Pierce sat on the side of the bed to receive her good morning kiss. 'Not today,' he mockingly refused as she would have pulled him down into the bed. 'I have to go out in a few minutes.'

Keeping silent wasn't one of her best qualities—as she had proved on more than one occasion!—but somehow she managed to do it this time. Disappointed as she may be at the thought of Pierce going out without her again she wasn't about to be accused of making 'whining complaints' again!

'Don't make your tongue bleed,' Pierce mocked. 'Hm?'

'You're biting down on your tongue so hard to stop yourself speaking, I thought you might hurt yourself,' he derided with amusement.

'Beast!'

He laughed softly. 'You know you love that particular part of my nature.'

She remembered every gentle caress, every fierce touch of the night before, knew that although Pierce had often been savage with her that there wasn't a bruise on her body, that the 'beast' in him was firmly controlled as he gave her pleasure beyond all imagination. 'And you enjoy the witch in me,' she huskily reminded him of the pleasure he had known in her caress.

He frowned as he noticed the subtle change in the statement. 'Does it still worry you that I can't love you?'

It was like asking her if she could be satisfied with the rainbow when she could have the crock of gold at the end of it! The rainbow was beautiful but it didn't last forever, as Pierce's attraction to her wouldn't.

'I don't worry about anything any more.' She spoke softly.

'Danielle——'

'Have you ordered breakfast yet?' she asked lightly. 'I have a fancy for strawberries. Have you noticed how well I'm adapting to being the mistress of a rich man?' she teased. 'I usually only have toast and coffee for breakfast, and then only if I have time.'

Pierce didn't smile. 'You aren't my mistress,' he rasped. 'You're a beautiful young woman who somehow finds something to love about me.'

'It's the dimples on your——'

'Danielle!' he warned softly, well aware of where the dimples were that she found so fascinating. 'Next time we turn off the light!'

'I like to look at you,' she told him gruffly. 'Maybe we could get one of those mirrors put over the bed at your house so that I——'

'And you call me decadent!' He stood up, shaking his head. 'You had better get up if you intend having breakfast with me; I have to leave in half an hour.'

'We had time after all!'

'Not for what I have in mind,' he growled, his eyes dark.

It was a strain being so teasingly cheerful all the time, and yet none of it showed when she joined him for breakfast ten minutes later, wearing her yellow sun-dress, her face bare of make-up, her hair secured in its single braid down her spine.

Pierce kissed her lightly before she sat down opposite him. 'What will you do with yourself today?' He watched her mockingly as she sprinkled a liberal amount of sugar on her bowl of strawberries.

She shrugged. 'I'll find something to do.'

He frowned. 'I don't want you to leave here.'

Danny nodded. 'Mm, these strawberries are delicious.' She licked the juice off her lips. 'Try one.' She spiked one of the fruits with her fork and held it out in front of him.

'Danielle——'

'Don't you like strawberries?' She frowned. 'I thought everyone liked them. They——'

'I *like* them!' He fiercely ate the red fruit. 'Danielle, I can't impress on you strongly enough——' He broke off as a knock sounded on the door. 'Danielle, I want you to——'

'Shouldn't you answer that?' she prompted as the knock sounded a second time.

Pierce glanced impatiently at his wrist watch. 'It's my car,' he realised abruptly, standing up to pull on his jacket. 'Stay in the hotel, Danielle,' he warned as he walked to the door.

'Taken for granted already,' she derided. 'No goodbye kiss,' she taunted as he frowned.

The kiss he gave her was distracted to say the least. 'You worry me,' he muttered.

'I do?' Her brows were raised.

'You do,' he said grimly. 'Poker last night, God knows what you'll get up to today!'

'Maybe I'll persuade Peter and Bob to take me to one of those bars where——'

'You will not!' Pierce told her gruffly. 'They have strict instructions to take care of you.'

She had already guessed that, just as she had guessed Pierce had been trying to obtain a promise from her that she wouldn't leave the hotel, which had been the reason she had constantly interrupted him; she couldn't possibly stay in this hotel suite, no matter how comfortable it was, all day. And she had no intention of dragging the two men he had left with her round on the sightseeing tour she intended taking. They had probably been to Washington hundreds of times before, would be bored by the whole thing.

She switched on the television programmes that never seemed to stop once Pierce had gone, inviting Bob and Peter into the lounge to have their breakfast. 'I'm going back to bed for a while,' she smiled.

Peter put down his coffee cup. 'I'll be just outside your bedroom door.'

'Please finish your breakfast,' she insisted with a beguiling smile.

'We're supposed to guard whichever room you're in,' Bob said firmly.

'You are guarding it,' she teased. 'From in here.'

'That isn't the way Mr Sutherland wants it,' he told her sternly.

Her smile remained in place with effort, already feeling closed in. 'It's only a matter of a few minutes,' she chided. 'You've almost finished eating.'

'I've finished,' Bob decided firmly. 'Peter will be in here, and I'll just be outside if you should need either of us.'

'But——'

'I know you think all this is unnecessary, Danny,' he sympathised. 'But this is the way Mr Sutherland wants things done.'

'Very well,' she sighed frustratedly, going through to the bedroom to sit on the bed impatiently twiddling her thumbs. This was intolerable. She wanted to see Washington. And, damn it, she was going to see it!

She marched over to the door, pulling it open. 'Bob, I'd like to go down to the shops.'

'Of course,' he nodded. 'I'll just tell Peter where we're going.'

She tapped her foot impatiently on the ground as she waited for him to talk to the other man, waiting until they reached the lift before making another move to get away. 'Oh, damn.' She pretended irritation. 'I've left my handbag in the bedroom; Bob, would you be a dear and get it for me?' She felt almost guilty about the money burning a hole in the pocket of her dress, Pierce insisting she take it yesterday.

He looked uncertain. 'If you'll just come back with me . . .?'

'I'll wait here,' she told him brightly. 'See,' she motioned towards the lift where the light indicated it was coming up to their floor, 'I'll stay here and hold the lift for us.'

He hesitated only a minute more before nodding abruptly. 'I'll only be a few seconds.'

Long enough for her to step lightly into the lift before it smoothly descended, going down to the floor beneath the main reception of the hotel to the desk where the tours were booedk, just managing to get on the bus that would take her to the Greyhound Bus Station where she could go on a conducted tour of Washington, having read about these arrangements in the hotel's brochure in the suite.

The White House looked much more impressive than it did on the television, the Lincoln and Jefferson Memorials much bigger than she had imagined, Abraham Lincoln looking as if he could get up out of the chair at any moment and address the people.

Danny decided to give the last port of call on the tour a miss, cemeteries not really one of her favourite places, even one as famous as the Arlington Cemetery where John F. Kennedy was buried. Instead, she took a taxi over to the Air and Space Museum, the woman at the booking desk having recommended it to her. And it wasn't difficult to see why, the exhibits of planes interesting enough in themselves, the rockets fascinating to look at.

It was only the hungry rumblings of her stomach that told her it must be getting late, although it took her several minutes to reverse the hours on her watch, having forgotten to adjust it to Washington time. Five-thirty. She had been out for hours, much longer than she intended; no wonder she felt hungry! She could only hope Pierce hadn't got back yet.

She felt the stirrings of unease when she stepped out of the elevator on their floor to find no one guarding the suite door. Although she instantly dismissed that, with Pierce not back yet, and her out too, there would be no one to guard.

She walked in to pandemonium, Don Bridgeman and Jerry Adams in the bedrooms on different telephones, Pierce pacing the lounge as he talked coldly to the two men seated in the room, a tall elderly man on the sofa, a brash-looking younger man in a chair. Pierce must have brought his business home with him.

His head snapped back as she entered quietly, the anger in silver eyes so intense that Danny thought for a moment he was going to hit her.

'I'll go in to the bedroom——'

'Danielle!' Pierce's voice cracked like a whip-end as he strode across the room to grasp her arm and swing her round. 'Where have you been?' he demanded fiercely.

'Sightseeing. Look, I'll leave you to finish your meeting, I didn't mean to interrupt. I'm sorry, gentlemen.' She gave the two men she didn't know a regretful smile.

'These *gentlemen* are policemen, Danielle.'

'There's nothing wrong is there?' she asked sharply. 'Cheryl and Nigel?' She looked up at Pierce apprehensively. 'My parents?'

The eldest policeman stood up. 'Would this be Danielle Martin, Mr Sutherland?' he said in a weary voice.

'Yes,' Pierce bit out with cold impatience.

'Pierce, is it Cheryl?' Danny was becoming alarmed by the situation.

'No, it's *you*, damn it,' he rasped harshly, his fingers tightly gripping her arm as he turned back to the policemen. 'It would seem I've been wasting your time, gentlemen,' he told them in a clipped voice. 'Miss Martin has merely been *sightseeing*!'

'Very well, sir,' the older man nodded, gesturing to his partner. 'We're glad everything worked out.'

Danny was still frowning once the two men had left. 'They were here because of me?'

'*Yes!*' Pierce released her only long enough to turn to the two guards he had in the suite, both of them off the telephone now as they stared at her sympathetically. 'You can go now,' he instructed harshly. 'Wait outside.'

Danny swallowed hard at the coldness in Pierce's voice, never having seen him quite this angry before. 'I'm sorry if I've caused trouble——'

'*Trouble!*' He swung away from her, his jaw clenched, his eyes blazingly angry. 'Where have you been all day?'

'Going round Washington.' She stated the obvious. 'I didn't realise what a fascinating city it is——'

'And if you walk in certain sections of it there's a chance you may not come out alive!'

'Oh, I haven't walked anywhere—well, only a little, in one of the park areas. I just couldn't believe how beautiful it all was. You hear all about Disneyland and places like that for holidaying in

America, but they don't really tell you about the elegance of Washington. The bus tour was so informative——'

'You've been on a bus?' Pierce asked with barely controlled violence.

'And in a taxi, to the museum, and another one back here.' She nodded. 'Everyone is so friendly——'

'My God, Danielle, do you have no sense at all?' he cut in fiercely. 'Anything could have happened to you while you've been happily wandering about the city.'

'Don't be silly, there were hundreds of women on their own like me——'

'*Not* like you,' he grated with suppressed violence.

'I'm really not that attractive, Pierce,' she scorned.

'To me you are,' he bit out. 'And by now a few people will have realised that. I went against my better judgment bringing you here in the first place.' He turned away. 'It was a mistake.'

'Just because I snuck off for a few hours to look at the city?'

'Because you tricked my security guards and went off alone!' he blazed.

Danny sighed. 'They make me claustrophobic.'

'Do you have any idea of the trouble you've caused?' he rasped coldly. 'I got back here at eleven-thirty to be told you had disappeared. Dawson left you at the lift for a matter of seconds and by the time he got back you had disappeared. We all thought you had been abducted. I've been going quietly out of my mind imagining what might have happened to you,' he recalled bitterly. 'The police assured me it was too soon to make assumptions, but I insisted you couldn't have gone off alone voluntarily.'

'Oh, Pierce, I'm sorry.'

He recoiled as if she had hit him. '*Sorry!*' he repeated furiously. 'Sorry isn't good enough, Danielle!'

'I really didn't mean to worry you.' She frowned at what she considered his unnecessary fury. 'But I'm back now, it's all over; I won't do it again.'

'You're right, you won't,' he ground out. 'We're all returning to England tomorrow.'

'You've finished your business?'

'Even if I hadn't we would be going back,' Pierce told her grimly. 'And I hope, for their sakes, that Dawson and Redman have left by the time we get back.'

'Bob and Peter . . .?'

'They're on their way back to England right now.' He nodded abruptly.

She swallowed hard. 'Because of me?'

'Of course,' he scorned. 'You've made a complete shambles of the security system that I felt was inviolate,' he said self-derisively. 'But in future any weak link I find in the system will be eliminated—immediately.'

'You've sacked two good men because I deliberately evaded them?' she said incredulously.

'It doesn't matter that you did it deliberately, it shouldn't have happened,' he bit out.

'You sacked them because of that? What sort of

man are you, Pierce?' Her temper rose. 'You destroy people's lives for no good reason——'

'I had a reason,' he stated flatly.

'Your damned paranoia!'

'Paranoid, am I?' His voice was steely. 'Let me tell you a little story, Danielle, and then perhaps you won't judge me as being such a cold-hearted bastard!'

'I didn't——'

'Just listen to me!' he grated fiercely. 'Sixteen years ago a young woman felt the same way that you do about security; she scorned it at every turn. But because she was married to a very rich man she was a target for any crazy idiot going. And no matter what you believe, there are thousands of them about!'

'Pierce——'

'Shut up and listen, damn you!' Pierce was suddenly dark and frightening. 'She found it great fun to give her bodyguard the slip, and did so at every opportunity, turning up hours later in a triumphant mood. Only one day she didn't come back. Several hours later her husband received a ransom demand. The money was paid but she was never handed over.'

Danny was very pale now. 'Pierce, please, I——'

'I gave them the money, Danielle.' He looked at her with tortured eyes. 'And they disappeared without giving us a hint of where we could find Sally.'

She had known he was talking about Sally, feeling his pain now as if it were her own. And she had called him paranoid, had once accused him of having no idea of the real world! He had suffered more than she would ever know.

'Two weeks later a teenage couple found her body in a deserted farmhouse in Wales,' he related flatly. 'The police believe she was dead before they even made the ransom demand.'

'Oh God, Pierce, don't go on,' Danny pleaded, never having seen such anguish in her life before as she could see in Pierce's eyes now as he relived the pain as if it were yesterday.

'I had to go and identify her body,' he continued as if Danny hadn't spoken. 'I hardly recognised her. She had been so beautiful, a black-haired gypsy, always laughing, completely full of fun. What I saw in the morgue was——'

'Pierce, no!' She ran to him, her arms about his waist as she hugged him tight, her face buried against his chest. 'Don't do this to yourself, darling. Please!'

'When I got back today and found you had disappeared I envisaged finding you the same way!'

'Oh *God*,' she choked, her arms tightening. 'I had no idea . . .'

'Of course you didn't.' His voice hardened, his hands steady as he pushed her away from him. 'You go through life doing exactly what you want.' He spoke dully. 'I have no right to try and stop that.'

'Pierce . . .?'

'I haven't been involved with a woman in this way since Sally died,' he told her flatly. 'I don't get involved, that way no one gets hurt. With you I've broken my own rules; it won't happen again.'

She swallowed hard. 'What do you mean?'

'Our—association, will end once we return to England,' he bit out, his eyes cold grey chips of ice. 'You will go back to doing exactly what you want, and I——'

'I won't let you shut yourself in behind those walls again,' she told him desperately.

'The choice isn't yours to make, Danielle,' he dismissed harshly. 'I was a fool to let you get even this close to me.'

'But you can't end things between us just because I didn't understand . . .'

'It isn't a question of what you understand, I do not get involved.'

'But——'

'I no longer want you in my life, Danielle,' he drawled. 'So you won't be allowed in it.'

He meant every word, she could see that. She hadn't known, how could she possibly have known! But she knew as far as Pierce was concerned that was no excuse; he meant it when he said he didn't get involved.

CHAPTER EIGHT

A PRISONER in her own bedroom, that was how she felt. And it wasn't even a bedroom she was sharing with Pierce. He had moved the things he needed for the night to the adjoining bedroom, making his plans clear. Don Bridgeman was outside the door to the corridor, Jerry Adams stood sentry at the door into the lounge.

She understood a little of what Pierce had gone through now, although no one could know the full extent of his suffering. But she still loved him, and she couldn't let him push her away just because he was frightened of being vulnerable a second time.

Her dinner had been sent in to her bedroom, and she knew Pierce intended keeping her here until they left for the airport tomorrow. She could hear Pierce in the adjoining bedroom and quickly took a shower before putting on a deep pink lacy nightgown she had brought with her, pulling on her black silky robe to hide the seductive diaphanous folds of the nightgown.

'Mr Sutherland said you were to stay in your room,' Jerry told her awkwardly as she stepped out into the lounge.

She gave him her most beguiling smile. 'I'm on my way to his room,' her husky voice gently mocked him.

'Oh.' He chewed indecisively on his inner lip. 'He didn't say anything about that.'

Obviously the instant dismissal of his colleagues had affected this man. 'I can assure you, Mr Sutherland didn't mean for you to keep me from his bedroom,' she said suggestively.

'I—Well, I—I'll just check with him.'

She had hoped to surprise a reaction from Pierce, but she didn't want to get anyone else into trouble, already guilty enough about Peter and Bob, although he knew by Pierce's mood this evening that she wouldn't change his mind about their dismissal the way he had Dave Benson. 'Please do,' she encouraged.

Jerry looked relieved that she hadn't taken offence, and knocking on Pierce's bedroom door, entered after being curtly told to do so. If Pierce humiliated her by saying no——

'You're to go straight in.' Jerry looked pleased that he had managed to do the right thing.

Pierce was seated at the ornamented desk in front of the window, coldly glancing up at her. 'Adams said you wanted to see me,' he rasped.

'Yes.' God, he was so remote. She couldn't believe she would be able to get through to this man.

'Well?' he prompted impatiently.

She untied her robe, holding the diamond pendant up in the palm of her hand. 'I came to return these——'

'I don't want them!'

'But——' She broke off, having looked up to meet the burning intensity of his eyes. He wanted her, in spite of himself, he still wanted her, looking hungrily at her body covered by the silky material of her robe.

Suddenly he shook his head, his mouth tightening. 'It isn't going to work, Danielle!'

She grimaced, knowing he had broken the mood—deliberately so. 'It isn't?'

'No!' He stood up, ruggedly handsome in a grey shirt and black trousers. 'I'm too damned old to be seduced by the sight of a female body!'

'Oh.'

His mouth twisted. 'Knowing your impetuous nature I don't suppose you have a back-up plan?'

She grimaced at his derision. 'This always works in films. After all, I do have a Raquel Welch figure!'

'Better,' he assured her tersely. 'But I've decided I'm in the mood for someone who looks a little more like Twiggy!'

Danny looked at him with reproachful eyes. 'That was cruel, Pierce. And unnecessary.' She spoke steadily, unclasping the necklace and taking off the earrings, placing them on the bed.

'Just as that was unnecessary,' Pierce ground out. 'I told you, they were a gift. They're yours.'

She gave a rueful grimace. 'I don't think I'd look right going to the local supermarket in them.'

'You could wear them anywhere you chose to!'

She shook her head. 'I don't want them——'

'Damn it, Danielle, I said they're a gift!'

'——because every time I looked at them I would remember your head against my breasts,' she finished quietly.

'God——!' Pierce closed his eyes briefly. 'Do you think I don't remember that, too?' he rasped, glaring at her. 'Do you think I don't want it, too?'

'Then why——'

'People get hurt when they love me, Danielle,' he rasped.

'You think I'll hurt any less loving you and not being allowed to be with you?'

'I will not risk another woman being harmed the way Sally was.'

'You can't stop me loving you, Pierce. I work on the estate, we'll see each other every day——'

'If you become too much of a nuisance I'll get rid of you,' he told her coldly. 'And you know that I'm capable of doing it, too.'

Yes, she knew, she knew that his will was inflexible. 'I love you, Pierce,' she said softly.

'I don't want you.'

'Liar!' she said instantly.

His mouth tightened. 'If you insist on staying in here tonight then I'll be forced into going out—and I can't guarantee I'll come back alone.'

Danny shook her head. 'You wouldn't do that to me.'

'I may not enjoy it, but I'd do it.'

She knew by the rigidity of his jaw that he would. He may have allowed her a brief insight into the softer side of his nature but it was definitely over. 'They say there's nothing worse,' she mused in a pained voice. 'Now I know how right they are.'

'They?' Pierce frowned his impatience with her cryptic comment. 'Right about what?'

Tears glistened in her sherry-brown eyes. 'There's nothing so sad as trying to rake over the embers of an old love affair,' she told him dully.

He sighed. 'Twelve hours isn't old.'

'It seems like a lifetime,' she choked.

'Danielle——'

'I'll be ready to leave in the morning,' she said sharply. 'I'm sorry I bothered you.'

'Danielle, for God's sake; I'm only thinking of you!'

She gave a bitter laugh. 'If you were thinking of me you would take me into your life and keep me there. You're trying to save yourself any pain, Pierce, not me.'

'After what I told you about Sally——'

'I feel sorry for you, very sorry for you,' she acknowledged tersely. 'But she's dead——'

'The men who did that to her aren't, though,' he ground out savagely.

'It's ridiculous to think they would come after me!'

'They won't be able to hurt anyone again when I catch up with them!'

'You're still looking for them?' Danny gasped. 'After all this time?'

He nodded grimly. 'I received information that one of them was in Washington.'

'That's the reason we're here?' she said disbelievingly.

'Yes. But I found out this morning the information was incorrect.'

This was what Nigel had wanted him to give up, what had obsessed Pierce for sixteen years. She had to agree with Nigel, it was self-destructive. It also sounded impossible if Pierce hadn't found the kidnappers after all these years of looking.

'Pierce, you have to give up this idea.'

'Not while they're still walking around,' he ground out determinedly.

'But——'

'Sally is dead,' he told her savagely. 'And I won't rest until I have her murderers.'

'But it's been sixteen years——'

'I don't care if it takes the rest of my life,' he rasped. 'I have to find them.'

She could see that he did, that he wouldn't find peace until he had. 'I understand.' She nodded dully. 'I'll go back to my room now.'

'You don't have to,' he told her wearily.

Her eyes widened. 'You want me to stay with you?'

'Why not?' He shrugged. 'We're already here together, one more night isn't going to matter.'

It mattered to her! 'I'm not one of your "conveniences", Pierce,' she bit out resentfully. 'I love you, but I won't be used.'

'Well, that's all it would be for me tonight.' He shrugged.

This time he wasn't even trying to deliberately hurt her, his memories too vivid for him to really want her. 'I'll see you in the morning,' she told him in a pained voice.

'Yes.' He nodded distantly. 'And, Danielle . . . I am sorry.'

So was she, sorry she couldn't have been the one to help him pass through the nightmare of the past, to show him that he could love again, had a right to live again, could find happiness with someone else. But he was so obsessed with avenging his wife's death he wouldn't allow love into his life again.

Life on the estate continued as usual, and even

Danny continued as usual, but it was no longer the same for her here, she could no longer feel the same contentment.

She heard Pierce leave and return in the helicopter with sporadic regularity, wondering how many of the trips were do to with Sally's death and not business. She saw nothing of the man himself, although she did try a couple of times to make her peace with him; she was always transferred to the estate manager.

Security around the house and grounds had been tightened, Don Bridgeman under sentence of instant dismissal if there were any more lapses like the ones Danny had caused. Maybe if she had known of Pierce's reason for such tight security she would have tried to . . . No, she knew she wouldn't have done anything differently. She couldn't live in a self-imposed prison the way Pierce did, she only hoped that he would one day realise he couldn't live that way any more, either.

She saw little of Cheryl and Nigel during the first few weeks of their marriage, understanding their need for privacy, finally inviting them down for dinner one evening shortly after they returned from a trip to America.

'Have you been raiding that food store again?' Cheryl teased as she ate the last delicious mouthful of the coffee gâteau they had had for dessert.

'Ssh,' Danny said playfully. 'Nigel thinks I did all this myself.'

'You mean you didn't?' Nigel said with feigned surprise.

'You told him!' Danny accused her sister.

'All I did was tell him to have something ready for indigestion if you had decided to cook the meal yourself,' Cheryl teased, more glowingly beautiful then ever.

'You aren't exactly the world's best cook!'

'Ah, but I no longer need to be,' Cheryl mocked.

'How did the move into your house go?' Danny asked interestedly as they all sat down in the lounge to drink their coffee, the newly married couple having decided to move out of Nigel's bachelor-flat and into a house of their own choosing. The fact that they had a live-in housekeeper and cook made Cheryl's lack of cooking skills irrelevant.

'It was a bit of a rush before we went away.' Cheryl shrugged. 'But it all looks wonderful.'

'Someone asked about you while we were away,' Nigel put in softly.

Danny frowned at him. 'But I don't know anyone in America.'

'Paul Banyon?'

She frowned at the speculative look in Nigel's eyes. 'Well, I did meet him briefly . . .'

'It may have been brief, but he assured me it was memorable,' Nigel drawled. 'Care to tell us about it?'

'No!'

His mouth quirked. 'I didn't think so. He was very disappointed you weren't there.'

'Where?' She frowned.

'His daughter's wedding,' Cheryl put in. 'I'm sure I told you that's the reason we were going to California.'

Danny was sure she had, too; she just hadn't been very attentive lately. 'Was it a nice wedding?'

His sister nodded. 'Clarissa looked like an angel. I've never seen a dress like it!'

'Darling, I'm sure your own dress is going to be spectacular,' Nigel put in indulgently, ruining the remark by adding drily, 'You've spent enough time at fittings for it!'

'Complaining already about how much you spend at the dressmaker, Cheryl,' Danny mocked. 'That's a bad sign.'

'Stirrer!' he muttered, turning to Cheryl. 'I was complaining about the amount of time you spend away from me,' he told her. 'Not the cost.'

'What a diplomat,' Danny chuckled.

'With a trouble-maker like you for a sister-in-law I have to be,' he said indignantly.

Her amusement increased. 'You shouldn't leave yourself so open.'

'Don't worry, darling.' Cheryl smiled at him. 'I know Danny's warped sense of humour too well.'

'I'm still waiting to hear how well she knows Paul Banyon,' Nigel taunted.

'I don't,' she answered awkwardly. 'I told you, I met him only once.'

'In that case he asked me some very strange questions about you.'

'What do you mean?' She frowned.

'He wanted to know if you still live at the bottom of Pierce's garden.'

She kept her expression deliberately bland. 'I don't see anything strange about that,' she dismissed. 'He knows I'm the gardener here.'

'He then asked if you still had the dogs with

you.' Nigel arched questioning brows. 'But you don't own a dog, do you, Danny?'

She blamed the colour in her cheeks on the heat of the room. After all, she never blushed, did she? 'You know I don't,' she mumbled, knowing what Paul Banyon had really been asking by those questions was whether or not she was still with Pierce!

'You could have come to California with us if you had wanted to see Paul again,' Cheryl told her questioningly.

'I hardly know the man.' She shook her head. 'And I have no idea what gave him the impression I would gate-crash his daughter's wedding.'

'He said he sent you an invitation.' Nigel frowned. 'But you declined to attend.'

She hadn't received any invitation. But she knew the reason she probably hadn't. 'The invitation was probably for Pierce and me.' Her voice was deliberately light. 'And he would have refused for both of us.'

'Oh dear.' Cheryl looked concerned. 'We hadn't thought of that. I'm so sorry, Danny——'

'Whatever for?' she chided dismissively. 'I never expected my relationship with Pierce to last.'

'But you loved him.' Her sister frowned.

'I still do,' she corrected. 'But he's created a vacuum for himself I just can't live in, and that he doesn't want me to share with him either. I understand about his wife now because he told me. It sounded awful.' She shuddered. 'But you can't go through life worrying if every person you meet is a possible threat to you.'

'It's the way he's lived since it happened,'

Nigel put in softly.

'I know that,' she sighed. 'But his obsession with finding the men that kidnapped Sally is totally senseless. If they haven't been found by now then they never will be.'

'Why do you say that?' Nigel asked softly.

'It's been sixteen years,' she dismissed. 'Those men have probably retired to a little island somewhere with their money and will never be seen again.'

'Unless they get greedy again,' he suggested.

'That isn't very likely!'

'Probably not,' he agreed distantly.

'Nigel——'

'How about making us all some more coffee, darling?' he firmly cut in on Cheryl. 'After all, Danny has been slaving over a hot oven all day!'

The subject of Pierce and his wife's death had been dropped by the time Cheryl returned with the coffee, Danny and Nigel discussing the wedding next month.

'Gary has agreed to come,' Cheryl told her huskily. 'And he's bringing one of the nurses from the hospital.'

Danny looked at her sister closely, seeing she was genuinely pleased that her ex-fiancé had decided to come to her wedding. The only trouble Danny could see concerned with the event was that she would have to see Pierce there, Nigel having asked his uncle to be his best man and been accepted. After Pierce's refusal to see her the last few weeks she knew he wouldn't be looking forward to having no choice about seeing her.

*   *   *

Who on earth could be banging on her cottage door this time of night? She blinked at the clock. It wasn't night at all, but six o'clock in the morning! Had something happened, to her family, to Pierce . . .?

She almost fell down the stairs in her haste, frowning up at Nigel as he stood on the doorstep, his appearance very rumpled, his clothes creased, his hair untidy. 'Cheryl . . .?'

'At home in bed by now, hopefully asleep now that she's made me come here and talk to you.'

'Come in.' She stepped back, tying the belt of her robe as she followed him in to the lounge. 'Can I get you some coffee?' she offered, still feeling half asleep.

'Maybe later,' he dismissed. 'It's about Pierce.'

'He's been hurt?' She paled. 'Tell me!'

'Calm down, Danny,' he soothed. 'As far as I know Pierce is at home asleep, too.'

She sighed her relief, sitting in the chair with her legs bent up beneath her. 'But something's bothering you about Pierce?' she prompted huskily.

Nigel grimaced, pacing the room. 'A guilty conscience.' He nodded. 'But I'd hoped——'

'Yes?'

He sighed. 'I'd hoped that being with you would stop Pierce on his road of vengeance. In fact, when he took you to Washington with him I was sure you meant more to him than any woman has since Sally; he never takes women with him on business trips.'

'It wasn't exactly business as it turned out,' she

said quietly. 'He was looking for Sally's kidnappers.'

'I was afraid of that last night, when you said he had told you about Sally,' Nigel said heavily.

'Yes?' She sensed he had something very important to tell her.

'I went to Germany last month,' he revealed slowly.

She remembered it—and the conclusion she and Pierce had come to about his subversive behaviour. 'You found them, didn't you?' She looked at him intently.

'I found—one of them. I think.'

'You think?' She stood up tensely.

'I can't be sure if it's him.' He grimaced. 'I didn't exactly speak to the man. But—there's quite a possibility that he was one of them.'

'Why didn't you tell Pierce about him?'

'Because I want it to stop!' he bit out forcefully. 'Do you have any idea what it's like to have watched him the last sixteen years, going round and round in circles, slowly destroying himself?'

'He has a right to know, Nigel,' she told him quietly. 'Whatever you found out you have to tell him; he isn't going to stop until he finds them.'

'The man is in prison,' he sighed. 'That's why I couldn't get to talk to him.'

Danny moistened her lips. 'What did he do?'

Nigel turned away. 'Shot someone.'

'Another woman?'

He shook his head. 'Something went wrong with the kidnapping plans, and he—he shot the woman's husband.'

'Wasn't once enough?' Danny groaned.

Nigel shrugged. 'Probably the money ran out. If you've done it once it must get easier.'

'How long has he been in prison?'

'About two years.'

She frowned. 'Then how did you find out about him?'

'Sources.' He pulled a face. 'Pierce has built up a lot of them over the years. The man got careless, talked to someone else about another kidnapping he committed years ago. When the other man got out he talked.'

'Then why wasn't Pierce the one to be told about it?'

'Because I was the one who got the report, not him. I thought it was just another of those false leads he's been getting since it happened, and I decide to save him another disappointment.'

'Only you weren't disappointed,' she realised heavily.

'No,' he acknowledged flatly. 'The information seems pretty sound. But if it is the man Pierce won't rest until he has him and his accomplices charged with Sally's death. And something like that could drag on for more years.'

'He'll never give up, Nigel.' She shook her head ruefully. 'Not while he has breath in his body. So you might as well save him any more senseless searching. You aren't doing him any favours by not telling him.' She touched Nigel's arm sympathetically.

'I had a feeling you would say that.' He pulled a face. 'So did Cheryl. You do realise he's likely to give me hell?'

She nodded. 'But explain to him why you did it,' she encouraged softly. 'Maybe he'll understand that you only tried to save him any more heartache.'

'He won't,' Nigel groaned. 'Have the coffee ready, hm?' he added heavily.

She drank two cups of coffee herself as she waited for him to come back, having no doubts that he would be able to get in to see Pierce.

She could understand why Nigel had acted as he had, would have been tempted to do the same thing herself in the circumstances. Although she knew Pierce wouldn't thank them for it!

It was almost an hour before Nigel got back, Danny was showered and dressed by that time, knowing she would sleep no more that morning. 'Coffee?' she asked in alarm as she saw how pale he was.

'Thanks.' He sipped the strong brew she had had waiting. 'Phew!' he finally sighed. 'Now I know what they mean by "tearing a strip off you"!' He grimaced. 'I feel raw!'

'Pierce was angry?'

'I'm surprised you didn't hear him over here!' Nigel admitted gruffly. 'Once I'd told him why I went to Germany he insisted I tell him everything. He is truly terrifying when he's in a rage like that.'

'And?'

'He thinks it could be the man, too,' Nigel sighed.

She chewed on her bottom lip. 'What's he going to do about it?'

Nigel looked up at her resignedly. 'He's going to Germany himself—right now.' He frowned as the helicopter could be heard leaving the estate.

CHAPTER NINE

THE days of waiting for Pierce's return were the worst Danny had ever known. And they were definitely the longest!

Surely he had to give up now, wouldn't try to have the man charged as Nigel thought he would? But remembering Pierce as she had last seen him he hadn't given the impression of giving up until justice was served. Until he was satisfied with that justice!

Perhaps Nigel had been right to try and keep the knowledge from Pierce, although she knew that it wasn't a decision they could make for him.

The evening of the fourth day she heard the return of the helicopter, knowing that didn't necessarily mean that Pierce was back, too, but going up to the house anyway, knowing as soon as she saw Don Bridgeman that Pierce *was* back.

'He said you were to go straight in.' Don opened the door for her and stood aside. 'He's in his study.'

'I know the way.' She nodded, not altogether surprised that Pierce had guessed she would want to see him, but a little stunned that he was allowing her to do so after his earlier rejection of her visits.

'Yes,' Don acknowledged.

She obeyed Pierce's terse instruction to enter after she had knocked on the study door, standing awkwardly in the middle of the room. If she

thought the ravages of the last weeks were
obvious on her she was shocked at how ill Pierce
looked. His eyes had a bruised sunken look, his
cheeks slightly hollow, very pale beneath his tan,
and he had obviously lost weight.

'Pierce . . .?'

'I'm all right, Danielle,' he dismissed her
concern harshly.

She wanted to go to him, to put her arms about
him and let him cry out his pain. But she knew he
didn't want that, that he would instantly reject
any sympathy from her. There was about him a
vulnerability, an air of emotional fragility that
would make him rebuff any act of human
kindness. He was like an angry animal who chose
to be alone to lick his wounds.

'Was it him?' she asked flatly.

'No,' Pierce rasped.

'It—it wasn't . . .?'

'No. Do you want a drink?'

'A small brandy—thank you,' she requested,
sitting down abruptly, sipping the fiery liquid,
not even noticing when it burnt her throat. 'Nigel
was so sure . . .' she said dazedly.

Pierce swallowed most of his own drink down
in one gulp, his expression bitter. 'He could have
saved himself the worry if he had just told me
sooner,' he rasped. 'He had no right to keep any
information from me.'

'He loves you——'

'He has a strange way of showing it!' Pierce bit
out angrily.

'If you could see yourself now you wouldn't
think so.' She shook her head sadly.

'What do you mean? he demanded sharply.

'Pierce, you look ill,' she told him pleadingly.

'So would you if you had met that animal and talked to him!' He stared straight ahead, his eyes not focusing on anything in the room, dull with pain. 'He killed a man, and yet he has no regret for what he did,' Pierce said disbelievingly.

'Tell me,' she encouraged softly, knowing he needed to talk.

'He has no conscience,' he rasped harshly. 'No feelings at all, that I could tell. He had carried out several other kidnappings, although not Sally's, thank God.' He was breathing heavily. 'I think I would have torn him apart with my bare hands if he had been the one who did that to her. It's the thought of the real culprit being an animal like that that's tearing me apart!' He groaned. 'I know her kidnappers were ruthless, but——'

'Pierce, sit down,' she urged, holding out her hand for him to come and sit beside her on the leather sofa, her fingers curling tightly about his as he did so. 'People like that have no emotions.' She looked at his drawn face worriedly. 'Darling, can't you see you have to let go of this,' she frowned. 'You can't keep searching for those men.'

'Let go?' His eyes blazed with emotion. 'I can't do that!' he bit out. 'It's at times like this that I feel capable of murder myself,' he added heavily.

Her eyes were wide. 'You—you wouldn't ever do anything that silly?'

'No,' he derided harshly. 'I wouldn't put myself on the same level as them. But I will see that they pay for their crime.'

'Haven't you already given enough years of your life trying to do just that?' she protested.

'As you once pointed out, I'm still young,' he told her flatly.

She swallowed hard, knowing he meant to go on. 'Sally wouldn't want——'

'How do you know what my wife would have wanted?' He turned on her angrily. 'I was married to her for over a year, I loved her, I think I'm in a better position to judge what she would have wanted than a young woman I shared a bed with for a brief time!'

Danny swallowed down the gasp of pain his cruelty evoked, knowing he was deliberately hurting her again. 'I'm sorry, Pierce.' She stood up abruptly. 'You're right, I couldn't possibly know what Sally would have wanted.'

'God, what am I doing?' he groaned, momentarily closing his eyes, a bright sheen added to their darkness when he lifted his lids. 'Danielle, I'm sorry.' He clasped both her hands. 'Don't go,' he pleaded.

'You need to be alone——'

'God, that's the last thing I need.' He looked tormented by memories. 'Stay with me tonight, Danielle. Take me into your generous warmth and show me that there is love in the world, that that brute wasn't a true example of humanity!'

She didn't care that it was just human comfort he needed from her, it was enough for now. 'Of course I'll stay with you, Pierce,' she assured him gently.

'Thank God for that.' He wrapped her in his arms, trembling slightly.

'Have you eaten?' She voiced her concern, wondering how often he had put himself through this same torture since Sally died.

'I'm not hungry,' he dismissed.

She looked up at him. 'Pierce, Sally died years ago, your not eating now isn't going to change any of that.'

He smiled bleakly. 'You sound like a mother talking to her little boy.'

She felt like his mother, wanted to protect him from any further pain. Wasn't that what they said about loving a man, that you became part mother, part lover, and part wife? She knew the joy and pain of the first two, the third would never be hers.

'When did you last eat?' she persisted.

'Yesterday, I think. Breakfast.'

'Then you're going to have dinner now,' Danny decided firmly.

'Yes, Danielle,' he agreed with mock meekness.

'And after dinner we're going for a short walk to clear away the cobwebs, and then we're going to bed.'

He frowned darkly. 'About going to bed . . .'

'I'm not expecting anything of you except your warmth,' she assured him softly, knowing that he was too full of memories tonight to think of any other woman but Sally. 'I just want to hold you.' She smiled gently.

He looked much better after he had eaten and the two of them strolled outside afterwards.

'How are you keeping yourself in shape nowadays?' he gently teased.

'I still jog.' She had her hand in the crook of his arm. 'I just use the country lanes now.'

Pierce frowned. 'Is that safe?'

She shrugged. 'There isn't much traffic.'

'I didn't mean from that sort of danger,' he rasped.

'Pierce,' she gently reprimanded, 'the reason you threw me out of your life——'

'I didn't throw you out!'

'—All right, asked me to leave——' she amended drily, 'was so that I wasn't a worry to you. It's my business if I choose to jog down country lanes.'

'It's irresponsible.' He scowled. 'You could get knocked over. Those lanes are hardly wide enough for cars, let alone a jogger, too!'

They both knew that wasn't the danger he feared. 'The lanes are pretty deserted at eleven o'clock at night.'

'Danielle . . .'

'Pierce!'

He drew in a ragged breath. 'Let's go back inside,' he suggested tersely.

She knew that the tense conversation had somehow changed things between them, that Pierce no longer wanted mere comforting but something else. And loving him as she did she couldn't deny him.

She turned straight into his arms when he joined her in the bed, their mouths fusing with desire and need, Danny's need as strong as Pierce's.

It was a magical night, the outside world forgotten amidst murmurs of delight, caresses that burned, bodies that melted into one, parting, only to come together again once more.

That closeness was broken as soon as Pierce told her the next morning that he was leaving.

'I'm going up to London for a while.' He touched her cheek gently as he lay in bed next to her.

She didn't ask why, knew that he needed to lose himself in work for a while. 'When will you be back?'

He shrugged. 'I'm not sure.'

She nodded, having already guessed that last night had changed nothing. 'I'd better get dressed then——'

'Danielle——' He broke off awkwardly, sighing deeply. 'You shouldn't have stayed with me last night, not once you realised I'd changed my mind about making love to you.'

'I love you.'

'Still?' He frowned.

'Always.'

Pain darkened his eyes. 'I care for you too much to want to hurt you, Danielle.'

'Then give up this madness,' she pleaded intently.

He moved away from her, both physically and mentally. 'I can't.'

'Pierce, if it were me,' she sat up on her knees, unconcerned with her nakedness, 'I wouldn't want you to keep punishing yourself like this. I'd want you to go on with your own life, accept that the past is over.'

'You don't understand,' he said soothingly, pulling on his robe. 'No one else understands.'

She wasn't reaching him, she doubted she ever would. 'I'd better go.' She stood up.

He looked at her with dark eyes. 'Be careful,'

he advised huskily.

She gave him a wan smile. 'I will. Please—take care, yourself.'

His smile was harsh. 'Don't worry about me, I'm the eternal survivor.'

She couldn't help worrying about him, about what he was doing to himself by this thirst for a revenge that was sixteen years old.

Cheryl and Nigel's church wedding was touchingly lovely, every mother's dream for a daughter, but although their vows were made with deep love for each other Danny felt sure their first wedding had meant just as much to them.

Danny watched Pierce during the ceremony, the first time she had seen him for three weeks. He looked more ill than ever, having lost even more weight, his face almost gaunt with strain.

'Looks terrible, doesn't he,' drawled a derisive voice.

Her eyes were wide as she turned, the buffet reception now in full swing. 'Paul Banyon!' she greeted warmly. 'I had no idea you would be here. Is Clarissa with you?'

'No,' he mocked. 'Since she discovered the joys of sex she and her husband rarely leave the bedroom!'

She couldn't help smiling. 'I'm glad it worked out for them.'

'And for Cheryl and Nigel too, by the look of them.' He glanced at the happy couple as they circulated among their guests. 'Only you and Pierce seem to be unhappy,' he added questioningly.

She accepted a glass of champagne off the tray one of her young cousins was taking round, sipping at it uninterestedly. 'We're friends,' she evaded.

'That's what I mean,' Paul mocked. 'Dare I hope that Pierce's loss is my gain?'

'Pierce hasn't lost,' she told him with simple honesty.

'Pity,' he drawled with regret. 'He obviously isn't appreciative of the fact.'

'Could we talk about something else?' she requested brittlely.

'Sure thing,' Paul agreed easily. 'How about my devastating charm?'

'Hm—how about it?' she derided, liking this man more than ever at their second meeting.

'Not working, hm?' He grimaced.

'Not particularly,' she laughed softly.

'Where are the dogs today?'

'With their handler, I would think.' She sobered. 'Probably outside somewhere,' she dismissed heavily, having been aware of the unobtrusive presence of Pierce's bodyguards both at the church and here at the reception. But she had expected that, knew Pierce never went anywhere without them. 'You have no bodyguards yourself?' she asked Paul curiously.

'I couldn't stand the restriction.' He grimaced. 'But we all know what Pierce went through with his wife; it's understandable it would have made him cautious.'

'You know about—Sally?'

He nodded. 'It was headlines at the time. The fact that she was found dead a couple of weeks later made smaller headlines, and eventually it was forgotten completely. Just another tragedy of the rich,' he said hardly.

'Not to Pierce.'

'She was his wife. Hell, if it had happened to my wife when we first got married I would have been pretty cut up about it, too. Probably after that as well; I may not be able to live with her but I wouldn't want to see her dead!'

'But——'

'You can never change a man's past, honey.' Paul squeezed her arm. 'You can only try to change the present. Now it seems to me that you and Pierce are just downright miserable apart.'

Pierce had said his search for Sally's murderers was private, and it seemed that it was; no one outside of his immediate family seemed aware of his continuing search.

'Pierce prefers not to have the responsibility of another person's emotions in his life,' she dismissed.

'I wouldn't have thought something like that would have bothered you,' Paul derided.

Danny frowned up at him. 'What do you mean?'

'The woman who burst through those doors that night with the dogs at her side didn't seem to me the sort that would give up. You were willing to fight for him then, why not now?'

Why not now?

Because Pierce didn't want her to! But in that she believed Pierce to be wrong, knew that he had to be made to forget the past, or if he couldn't forget it to at least accept it.

'Thank you, Paul.' She reached up and kissed

him warmly. 'I was confused for a while, believed I had to accept Pierce's rejection. But I don't, not while I know he still wants me. He can push me away all he wants in future, but I'm going to fight for him.' Nothing had changed since the night she had been prepared to fight another woman for him, it was only her adversary that had changed.

'You can start right now,' Paul murmured. 'He's coming over.'

She turned to see Pierce fast approaching them, a grim tightness to his mouth.

'Paul,' he greeted the other man stiffly. 'I hadn't realised the two of you had kept in touch.'

'Oh, Danny and I are the best of friends,' Paul told him blandly.

'I see,' Pierce rasped.

'I doubt it,' Paul mocked with amusement. 'I hope you'll both excuse me while I go and congratulate the happy couple.' He touched Danny's cheek gently. 'I'll see you later.'

After he had gone Danny and Pierce stood side by side, neither of them speaking. Finally she could stand it no longer. 'It was a lovely wedding, wasn't it?'

'Yes.'

'You made a nice speech,' she told him lightly.

'Thank you. You look beautiful in that lilac gown.'

'Thank you.'

'Danielle.' His gaze was suddenly intent. 'I don't think you should become involved with Paul.'

Her heart gave a leap, never dreaming that her method of fighting lay in a jealousy she hadn't even guessed at. But Pierce was jealous of Paul, she could see it by the angry blaze in his eyes. 'Why not?' she asked softly.

'The man is a flirt. He——'

'Why should that bother you?' She frowned.

'It doesn't bother me,' he dismissed harshly. 'I just don't want to see you get hurt.'

'Again, you mean?'

'Danielle, I never meant to hurt you.'

'But you did.'

'I warned you not to love me.'

'Can I help it if my heart didn't listen?'

Pierce gave a heavy sigh. 'I should never have become involved with you.'

'No,' she acknowledged lightly.

He gave her a sharp look. 'You agree?'

'Mm.' She nodded.

Pierce looked suspicious now. 'You accept that our becoming lovers was a mistake?'

'I didn't say that.' She shook her head. 'I don't regret loving you.'

'Danielle, I'll never allow myself to love you in return,' he grated.

She knew that was the problem. It wasn't that he couldn't love her, he just *wouldn't* let himself.

'Pierce.' She touched his arm. 'I understand all the problems involved in it, but today I decided I'm going to marry you. Maybe I'll have to wait until we're both old and grey, but one day you'll realise that you just can't do without me. I'm going to be living in that cottage at the bottom of your garden until you find you can't stay away any longer.'

He swallowed hard. 'I'll never love you.'

'Won't you?' She smiled gently.

'No!'

'Then it won't bother you that Paul is staying at the cottage with me tonight,' she dismissed, knowing that if she asked him the other man would do just that.

Steely fingers clamped about her arm. 'You wouldn't do that,' he grated.

'Why not?' She shrugged. 'I'm going to marry you, Pierce, and I'll wait a lifetime to do it, but I didn't say I would wait alone.'

'Danielle!' He held on to her as she would have walked away from him.

'Yes?' She quirked light brows, wondering if these actions were worthy of the woman with the dogs. Then her actions had been completely honest; she couldn't say the same about what she was doing now.

'Damn you!' Pierce released her, striding away, his back rigid.

CHAPTER TEN

SHE shouldn't have challenged him in that way; he wasn't ready for this yet. And if he didn't come to the cottage tonight, allowed the night to pass believing she was spending it with Paul, then she knew there was no hope for them. It was too soon for him, damn it, *too soon!*

Standing in her darkened bedroom she could see the lights on around the pool, knew that Pierce must be gliding smoothly through the water. It was after eleven now; would he come to her or would he vent his anger by swimming until he dropped? She had gambled much too soon, and her impetuosity could be the end for her this time.

She wandered back downstairs, too restless to sleep, wishing she could find something to do to take her mind off Pierce. Mowing the lawn was certainly out of the question tonight!

She was on her third cup of coffee when she heard a noise outside followed by a loud thumping on her back door. Pierce had come!

'All right, where is he?' Pierce pushed past her into the cottage as soon as she opened the door, wearing brief black swimming trunks. His eyes narrowed on her as she stood before him in her bare feet—the cotton nightgown that covered her from neck to foot was hardly provocative.

'Ssh,' she urged softly. 'You'll wake——'

'I'll do more than wake him when I get hold of him,' Pierce warned her savagely.

'—my parents,' she finished ruefully.

He frowned, looking disbelieving. 'Your parents are staying with you?'

Danny nodded. 'Upstairs in the spare bedroom.' She frowned as she touched his bare arm. 'Darling, you're frozen!' she realised. 'Didn't you dry yourself after your swim?'

'The air dried me on the way over here,' he replied uninterestedly. 'I want——'

'You'll catch pneumonia,' she scolded, leaving the room to get him a towel, almost walking into him as she turned to find he had followed her. 'Here.' She held out the towel to him.

'Are you sharing a bed with Paul while your parents are here?' he grated.

'Yes and no.' She took the towel off him and wrapped it about his shoulders as he made no effort to do anything with it, briskly rubbing his cold flesh.

'Yes and no what?' he demanded, impatiently pushing her hands away from him.

'Yes, my parents are in the house, and no, I'm not sharing a bed with Paul.'

'But you told me——'

'Yes?'

'You lied to me.' He scowled.

She sighed, shaking her head. 'I asked if it would bother you if Paul stayed at the cottage tonight; it obviously did, so he hasn't.'

His eyes were narrowed. 'Did you ever intend to go to bed with him?'

'No,' she answered truthfully. 'Please don't be

angry, Pierce! I was only trying to show you that you *do* care about me.'

'I know I *should* be angry with you,' he groaned, his arms coming about her. 'But I'm too relieved that it isn't true about you and Paul to feel anything else. You're right, Danielle, I do love you. And the thought of any other man touching you fills me with murderous rage!'

And the possession in his voice filled her with delight! She melted against him, her arms about his neck. 'The thought of any other woman touching you fills me with the same rage,' she told him throatily.

'There haven't been any other women, not since the first night I made love to you,' he assured her huskily, releasing the buttons down the front of her nightgown. 'And I thought this was a little too modest for the seduction you seemed to have in mind tonight!' he derided as he bared her breasts and the gentle slope of her stomach and hips.

She smiled a secret smile. 'I wore it hoping you would come here tonight.'

He frowned down at her. 'You knew I would?'

'I had to hope, Pierce.' She shrugged. 'If you hadn't . . .'

'Then your plans would have gone all wrong,' he finished mockingly. 'Darling, I'm not angry.' He smoothed the frown from her brow. 'These last few weeks without you have been hell.'

'Your weight loss . . .?'

'How could I eat when I wanted to be with you?' He sighed. 'Someone had to bring me to my senses; I'm glad it was you. I've done a lot of thinking since we parted, about Sally's death, the years since, the changes in me. I used to be like you, Danielle, resentful of any restrictions to my movements. I think that's why I was never really angry with Sally when she managed to get away from it all.'

'Pierce, I'll have a bodyguard if it will make you happy,' she hastily assured him, knowing that she would do anything to give him peace of mind now that she knew what he had gone through in the past. 'If Princess Diana can get used to it so can I,' she added ruefully.

'I'm sure you would.' He smiled at her attempt to lighten his tension about the subject. 'But I know you would hate it. And while I can't dispose of the security altogether,' he added before she could say anything, 'I'm willing to compromise—slightly—where you are concerned.'

'In what way?' She frowned.

'How would you feel about an Alsatian pup, one of Ferdinand and Kilpatrick's brothers about six litters further on? You have a way with the dogs, and Danton could train him for you.' Pierce looked at her anxiously.

It was a *big* compromise on his part, and she eagerly accepted. 'I'll have to think of a suitable name for him. How about Attila, or Genghis?'

Pierce laughed softly, obviously relieved by her reaction. 'I think I prefer Rover!'

'No imagination,' she chided.

His humour faded. 'I hadn't finished,' he warned softly. 'While you're in the grounds the dog will be adequate protection, but if either of us goes further than that, a human guard goes with us.'

'Just one?'

He sighed. 'Just the one,' he conceded. 'My actions concerning security may have been extreme in recent years, but I don't believe in stupidity.'

That she had achieved even this much, when she could have lost it all on a gamble, filled her with relief.

'Sally's death shook me up, badly,' he admitted tensely. 'And as the years passed I found it easier just having to worry about myself, didn't want the responsibility of anyone else, I realise that now. But I wanted you from the first, knew I had to have you. It wasn't until that night you came to the house expecting to have to keep me out of Clarissa's arms that I even began to suspect I could be falling in love with you. And even when I did I couldn't stay away from you. You were magnificent that night, like a goddess come to claim her lover; I just hadn't realised how badly I wanted to be claimed. But I knew in Washington,' he rasped bitterly.

'Pierce——'

'While you were missing that day it was worse than anything—*anything*—I'd gone through before.' He looked at her with pained eyes. 'The years since Sally died have been a self-punishment, denying myself love. But even with you out of my life I've worried about you, wanted to keep you safe. But my guilt about Sally held me back——'

'Darling, you didn't kill Sally just because you

loved her, just as she didn't die because she loved you. She was killed by something beyond your control . . .'

'Because she was my wife!'

'She could have been killed walking in front of a bus,' Danny protested. 'Hiding in a house during a storm isn't going to help you if a tree falls on the house,' she reasoned. 'You can't hide from the dangers of life, you can only respect them.'

'Wise Danielle.' He gently touched her lips. 'Knowing instinctively what it's taken me sixteen years to realise.'

'What will you do about those men now?'

He sighed. 'I'd like to say I'll give up looking, but I know I'd be lying. But it won't dominate my life—our lives.'

She appreciated his honesty, knew that he couldn't give up his search completely. 'That's all I ask,' she assured him softly.

'And all I ask is that you marry me and go on loving me for the rest of our lives.' He looked at her intently.

Not an impossible dream at all, but a possible reality!

Danny wasn't even conscious of the mower in front of her as she walked up and down cutting the grass, all of her thoughts with Pierce and the two men he had with him in the lounge.

The two policemen had arrived before Pierce returned from his business meeting, and for half an hour she had sat and entertained the two stone-faced men, apprehensive about the reason they wanted to see the man who had been her husband for the last three years.

They had been married in the same church as Cheryl and Nigel only two months after them. The last three years had been good ones, happy years together, and at times she would swear Pierce had forgotten Sally's tragic death for weeks at a time. But the appearance of those two policemen worried her.

She turned off the mower to walk across the garden, the faithful Nelson at her side. He had come to her at only a few months old, had been trained by Danton and herself to protect her, something he did without hesitation. He was also the family pet, and Danny knew Pierce loved him as much as she did.

She glanced back at the house. Today had been going to be a good day for them, but the news those two policemen brought boded ill for that. She had been aware of Pierce's continuing search for Sally's murderers, but it hadn't intruded on their life together. Pierce was almost a different man from the coldly withdrawn one she had first met. Her mother and father adored him. Cheryl and Nigel's two children, a boy of two called Nathan, and a little girl of one called Amy, thought their Uncle Pierce was tremendous fun, looking forward to their visits here. Their own happiness together had been beyond question, and . . .

'What are you doing all the way over here?' Pierce looked down at Danny as she sat beneath the big oak tree, Nelson sitting watchfully at her side.

Her gaze was apprehensive as he sat down on the grass beside her. 'Your visitors have gone?'

'Yes. I'm sorry you were troubled with them this afternoon. I had no idea——'

'They've found them, haven't they?' she said quietly.

'One of them,' he confirmed softly, taking her hand in his. 'The other one is dead. You remember the Robbins kidnapping?'

About two months ago the young bride of the industrialist George Robbins had been abducted, thankfully she had managed to escape unharmed. Danny nodded.

'Apparently the police considered the similarity between the two cases too great to be ignored, and when they caught the two men who kidnapped Rebecca Robbins they pressed for charging them with Sally's kidnapping, too. It took three days, but one of them finally confessed. It seems his original partner died of a heart attack over five years ago.'

'I'll pack you a bag,' she told him huskily.

Pierce shook his head. 'I'm not going anywhere.'

Her eyes widened. 'But——'

'Danielle, the man has been charged, his partner is dead, there's nothing more I can do.'

'But don't you want to be there, to . . .'

'No.' He gathered her into his arms. 'The man has been caught, the law can deal with him now.'

She gave a choked cry of relief as she clung to him. 'I thought . . .'

'I know what you thought.' He stroked the silky softness of her hair. 'But I only wanted the men to be caught, Danielle, I no longer want personal revenge against them. It's over, darling.'

Her relief was immense, having imagined Pierce would be rushing up to London immediately, that he would be there for months while the court case against the men went on.

'Nelson is getting jealous,' Pierce finally drawled as she still clung to him.

She shook her head. 'He knows better. It's only if *other* men touch me that he gets worried.'

'There are no other men,' Pierce claimed arrogantly.

'You're only saying that because you know it's true,' she teased.

He nodded. 'And because after three years you still make it impossible to leave our bed in the mornings.'

She laughed softly. 'And you very often don't.'

'No,' he acknowledged ruefully.

'Darling, I have some news myself,' she told him huskily.

'Mm?' He played with the lobe of her ear.

'You're going to be a father.'

He looked down at her with raised brows. 'Already?'

They had made a conscious decision to have this baby, and three months ago had dispensed with the use of precautions. 'Unfair, isn't it?' She wrinkled her nose. 'I thought we could have lots more months of fun before I became pregnant.'

'We still can,' Pierce assured her throatily. 'I've heard pregnant women can be very sexy.'

'From Nigel, no doubt,' she derided, knowing

the two men often played golf together. 'I suppose that's his excuse for there only being ten months between Nathan and Amy!'

'Probably,' Pierce chuckled, looking down at her wonderingly. 'You're sure about the baby?'

'Well the doctor is, so I suppose I'd better be,' she mocked.

'You're pleased?'

She smoothed the anxiety from his brow. 'Very,' she assured him emotionally. 'I can't wait to have your baby.'

'Well, it doesn't look as if you're going to have to,' he teased. 'I can't tell you how happy you've made me——'

'Hey, we made this baby together,' she chided softly.

'I don't just mean the baby.' He looked at her intently. 'The three years I've had with you have been the best years of my life. The most erotic too,' he added ruefully.

'Love is an eroticism in itself.' She pulled his head down to hers. 'When you love you want to please.'

Pierce kissed her lingeringly. 'You please me to the point of insanity sometimes,' he admitted gruffly.

'Now?'

'Yes,' he acknowledged softly.

She stood up, pulling him agilely to his feet. 'Then let's go home.'

They walked towards the house, arms around each other, the faithful dog at their heels.

'An ending and another beginning,' Pierce murmured huskily, his hand resting protectively on the flatness of her stomach that would soon grow big with his child.

Danny understood that he had finally said goodbye to the past, that their future and the future of their child was all that mattered to him now.

Harlequin *Presents*

Coming Next Month

895 STORM Vanessa Grant
After being stranded by a fierce storm in the Queen Charlotte Islands a reporter doubts herself, the hard-hitting pilot she desires and her commitment to a childhood sweetheart.

896 LOSER TAKE ALL Rosemary Hammond
A wealthy American doesn't exactly win his new bride in a poker game. But it amounts to the same thing, because it's marriage for them—win or lose!

897 THE HARD MAN Penny Jordan
Desire for a virtual stranger reminds a young widow and mother she is still a woman capable of love, capable of repeating the mistake she made ten years ago.

898 EXPLOSIVE MEETING Charlotte Lamb
A lab technician's boss resents his employee's impassioned plea on behalf of a brilliant scientist who keeps blowing up the lab. And he misinterprets her persistence—in more ways than one!

899 AN ALL-CONSUMING PASSION Anne Mather
When her father's right-hand man comes to the Caribbean to escort the boss's daughter back to London, she tries to make him forget his responsibilities—never thinking she is playing with fire.

900 LEAVING HOME Leigh Michaels
A young woman never dreams her guardian's decision to remain single had anything to do with her, until he proposes marriage—to pull her out of yet another scrape.

901 SUNSTROKE Elizabeth Oldfield
Can a widow reconcile receiving twenty thousand pounds to pay off her late husband's creditors with leaving the man she loves—even though he's been groomed to marry someone else?

902 DANGEROUS MOONLIGHT Kay Thorpe
It is possible that the Greek hotel owner a vacationer encounters isn't the same man who ruined her sister's marriage. But can she risk asking him outright, when the truth could break her heart?

Available in July wherever paperback books are sold, or through Harlequin Reader Service.

In the U.S.
901 Fuhrmann Blvd.
P.O. Box 1397
Buffalo, N.Y. 14240-1397

In Canada
P.O. Box 2800, Postal Station A
5170 Yonge Street
Willowdale, Ontario M2N 6J3

Can you keep a secret?

You can keep this one plus 4 free novels

Janet Dailey
Americana

A romantic tour of America with Janet Dailey!

Enjoy the first two releases of this collection of your favorite previously published Janet Dailey titles, presented alphabetically state by state.

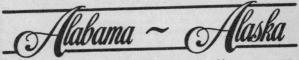

Alabama ~ Alaska

One of America's best-selling romance authors writes
her most thrilling novel!

TWIST OF FATE

JAYNE ANN KRENTZ

Hannah inherited the anthropological papers that could
bring her instant fame. But will she risk her life and give
up the man she loves to follow the family tradition?

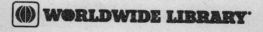

Harlequin Intrigue

**Because
romance
can be quite
an adventure.**

Available wherever paperbacks are sold or through

Harlequin Reader Service

In the U.S.
901 Fuhrmann Blvd.
P.O. Box 1325
Buffalo, N.Y. 14269

In Canada
P.O. Box 2800, Station "A"
5170 Yonge Street
Willowdale, Ontario M2N 6J3

INT-6R

Harlequin "Super Celebration" SWEEPSTAKES

NEW PRIZES—NEW PRIZE FEATURES & CHOICES—MONTHLY

1. To enter the sweepstakes, follow the instructions outlined on the Center Insert Card. Alternate means of entry, NO PURCHASE NECESSARY, you may also enter by mailing your name, address and birthday on a plain 3" x 5" piece of paper to: In U.S.A.: Harlequin "Super Celebration" Sweepstakes, P.O. Box 1867, Buffalo, N.Y. 14240-1867. In Canada: Harlequin "Super Celebration" Sweepstakes, P.O. Box 2800, 5170 Yonge Street, Postal Station A, Willowdale, Ontario M2N 6J3.

2. Winners will be selected in random drawings from all entries received. All prizes will be awarded. These prizes are in addition to any free gifts which might be offered. Versions of this sweepstakes with different prizes may appear in other presentations by TorStar and their affiliates. The maximum value of the prizes offered is $8,000.00. Winners selected will receive the prize offered from their prize package.

3. The selection of winners will be conducted under the supervision of Marden-Kane, an independent judging organization. By entering the sweepstakes, each entrant accepts and agrees to be bound by these rules and the decision of the judges which shall be final and binding. Odds of winning are dependent upon the total number of entries received. Taxes, if any, are the sole responsibility of the winners. Prizes are not transferable. This sweepstakes is scheduled to appear in Retail Outlets of Harlequin Books during the period of June 1986 to December 1986. All entries must be received by January 31st, 1987. The drawing will take place on or about March 1st, 1987 at the offices of Marden-Kane, Lake Success, New York. For Quebec (Canada) residents, any litigation regarding the running of this sweepstakes and the awarding of prizes must be submitted to La Regie de Lotteries et Course du Quebec.

4. This presentation offers the prizes as illustrated on the Center Insert Card.

5. This offer is open to residents of the U.S., and Canada, 18 years or older, except employees of TorStar, its affiliates, subsidiaries, Marden-Kane and all other agencies and persons connected with conducting this sweepstakes. All Federal, State and local laws apply. Void where prohibited or restricted by law. Winners will be notified by mail and may be required to execute an affidavit of eligibility and release which must be returned within 14 days after notification. Winners consent to the use of their name, photograph and/or likeness for advertising and publicity in conjunction with this and similar promotions without additional compensation. One prize per family or household. Canadian winners will be required to answer a skill testing question.

6. For a list of our most recent prize winners, send a stamped, self-addressed envelope to: WINNERS LIST, c/o Marden-Kane, P.O. Box 525, Sayreville, NJ 08872.

No Lucky Number needed to win!